Birth of a Terrorist

Nick Morrow

Order this book online at www.trafford.com
or email orders@trafford.com

Most Trafford titles are also available at major online book retailers.

This book is a work of fiction, any resemblance to names, places, cultures and area settings are coincidental.

Note for Librarians: A cataloguing record for this book is available from Library
and Archives Canada at www.collectionscanada.ca/amicus/index-e.html

Printed in Victoria, BC, Canada.

ISBN: 978-1-4251-5184-3 (soft)
ISBN: 978-1-4269-1322-8 (hard)
ISBN: 978-1-4251-5186-7 (ebook)

Library of Congress Control Number: 2009931985

*We at Trafford believe that it is the responsibility of us all, as both individuals
and corporations, to make choices that are environmentally and socially sound.
You, in turn, are supporting this responsible conduct each time you purchase a
Trafford book, or make use of our publishing services. To find out how you are
helping, please visit www.trafford.com/responsiblepublishing.html*

*Our mission is to efficiently provide the world's finest, most comprehensive
book publishing service, enabling every author to experience success.
To find out how to publish your book, your way, and have it available
worldwide, visit us online at www.trafford.com*

Trafford rev. 7/21/2009

 www.trafford.com

North America & international
toll-free: 1 888 232 4444 (USA & Canada)
phone: 250 383 6864 ♦ fax: 250 383 6804 ♦ email: info@trafford.com

I dedicated this book to my wife Marie Rose Aline, the South Wind that filled my sails in sometimes-dead seas, drifting me closer to an invisible horizon.

Also, Alex Myers and her mother Renee, they sprinkled compliments when all was dry and unforgiving.

Last but certainly not least, to all the loving peoples of the world who instinctively hold a child to their chest, letting it remember their beating heart forever through its lifelong journey.

Nick Morrow,

December 2008.

Prologue.

In our worlds misty past, all cultures created religions that try to focus their followers' vision on a better world, by creating high moral values, do not lie, cheat, steal or take others lives.

These values intend to lead their followers away from harmful deeds, to follow a path of goodness.

Many agree it is necessary to manage the undisciplined mind harboring selfishness and other attitudes that could be sources of trouble. All point to a state of mind that is peaceful, disciplined, ethical, and wise.

We should not judge cultures unless they are destructive to humanity from religious differences rising 1from cultural dogma.

There are groups that modify religious beliefs to justify their personal need for a closure whether it is anger or a corruption by power.

These modifications have a magnetic effect on other people who need closure for personal anger and raise the levels of their failing self-esteem. This creates a chain leading off into the distance, lying in wait for the unborn.

Children in all cultures are born innocent and very susceptible to imprinting by its parents or caretakers.

At birth, a process begins to provide the basics, food, clothing, and shelter.

Affection in some cases neglected due to previous similar conditioning by a parent or caretaker. Physical and/or emotional abuse replaces the necessary, love and affection. Cultures may differ but a newborn infant's mind is submissive in all humans.

The impressionable infant molds into a villain with similar needs as its parent or caretaker.

The world is an imperfect place with sometimes-unbroken circles. The majority of children in all cultures are born innocent and provided with a gentle understanding of the world. Some infants through emotional and physical abuse develop an anger that has a hunger, a need to continue their chain of abuse to others.

The human mind is the engine of its body and in most societies, neglected.

Humanity struggles to find cures for anatomical afflictions, but through a lack of understanding, emotional afflictions become neglected.

This imperfection in humanity creates an environment that affects all cultures; they become victims of their own creations.

There exists a solution for the world's imperfection; it waits unnoticed.

The solution is "Love conquers all."

Nick Morrow.

December 2008.

CHAPTER – 1

Saleem Mohammad dal Figar stood and watched as the same uncontrollable rage invaded his father. A familiar, fear was rising in his body also, he remembered the times his father had lost control and beaten him. Saleem remembered a simple, childhood act that had reduced the tempo of the beating. He would kneel on the floor, press his head to the carpet, and cover his head with his hands.

For the father, this vision of his child in this submissive position possibly had some effect of cooling the flames of his anger. He would slowly reduce beating the child, step back and continue shouting until there was an unknown closure for the emotional explosion. The volume and tempo of shouting slowly died away, and then he would leave the terrified child to recover.

This day was to be destiny, Saleem had grown into a young man, a different kind of chemistry flowed through his body.

Saleem stood and looked into his father's face, the violence inside had come out in a blood red color, this color overflowed into the man's eyes making them red rimmed also. He stood facing his father's rage.

He could feel his father clutching the front of his shirt, his fist pushing into his chest causing rising pain. Saleem felt something break inside of him, the bond between father and son finally broke, and years of punishment finally took its toll. In addition, the childhood instinct to fall to the floor did not come to his rescue.

Suddenly, hot anger from inside of Saleem, forced his arms up, he grabbed the front of his father's shirt and pulled him suddenly forward, then opening the palms of his hands, he pushed as hard as his grown body would allow. The force tore Saleem's shirt, the front of it stayed in his father's clenched fist.

His fathers staggered backwards, almost falling, then adjusting his legs and posture, he remained upright. He stood and looked at Saleem; his eyes had the yellow glow of a predator. Father and son stood this way for what seemed like eternity; suddenly his father took a step forward and struck Saleem across the face with the back of his hand.

The blow had tremendous force, starting at the waist, backed by powerful shoulders and transferred to a thick forearm; it knocked the young man backwards onto the carpet. A huge, diamond ring on his father's hand ripped Saleem's cheek open, revealing white bone.

Lying on the floor, bleeding, Saleem could feel a hot fire rising inside of him; it scorched and destroyed any fragments of love or affection he had ever felt for his father. A need to rise and get justice for himself suddenly rose in his body. Turning on his side, he raised himself on one arm, instinct made him look up at his father, he saw a complete transformation in his face, it had turned white. Saleem sat on the floor looking at this change from rage to possible white-faced guilt.

It could have been the first blood running down Saleem's chest, onto the carpet. The cut on Saleem's check was deep from the diamond ring on his father's hand, releasing a great volume of blood. He stood looking at his son covered in blood, his eyes shifted in what could have been an accumulated burden of guilt. He looked away, turned, and without a word walked out of the room.

The flight from Frankfurt to Seattle, Washington was long and tedious, the huge, silver jet filled with exhausted passengers, seemed to hang suspended in the night sky. Many were sleeping, covered with airline blankets; some were reading under dim overhead lights, and others had headsets on, watching onboard television. Through the airliner's oval windows, the view of the night was magnificent. Glow from a majestic, silver moon touched peaceful, sleeping faces. Stars glittered in the midnight colored sky; it was a scene of peace.

A female flight attendant slowly walked down the aisle toward the rear of the plane. Glancing from side to side, she checked for passenger comfort, fallen articles, or general problems that could exist. Shirley West had developed a subconscious ability to relax after the frantic pace of serving meals and drinks. As she walked down the aisle, her whole body was finally at rest, her eyes however, never rested, they were always searching. This process seemed to require very little effort, allowing Shirley to enjoy the peace of the moment.

A slim, elegant woman, Shirley moved down the aisle with feminine grace and a gentle rolling motion of her trim hips. Short, black hair and fashionable glasses complimented her high cheekbones; in short, Shirley West was a good-looking woman. Sincere and romantic, she loyally tended her fires of passion, but still could not hold a relationship with a man. Shirley wondered if the job kept her away from home too much. She loved her job, so she wished the right man would come along, he would be the solution to her loneliness. Many times, when she lay in bed, alone and lonely, her sadness would come and search for the answer, Shirley would fall asleep and dream of better times.

As she walked, her restless eyes searched for the handsome, male passenger sitting in an aisle seat. Shirley saw him lean over and pick up an airline blanket that had fallen on the floor. The man stood up and gently placed it back on a grey-haired woman sleeping in the aisle seat across from him. The act touched Shirley; a soft, warm glow of emotion flowed through her.

He was a handsome man with dark, short, hair that blended with his darker skin tones. A white scar running down his cheek added to the aura of mystery and enhanced his masculinity. He had large, brown eyes with mysterious, liquid depths. Shirley had looked into them and something stirred inside of her. She noticed him more often after that, glancing out of the corner of her eye as she passed on her rounds. On one occasion, their eyes met and instead of the aggressive, penetrating, masculine look, he dropped his eyes, breaking contact, Shirley liked him even more.

Walking slowly down the aisle toward his seat, she saw the man finish tucking the blanket gently around the sleeping woman then return to his seat. Shirley stopped beside the man. "You are very kind," she said. He looked at her for a second, then his eyes dropped, she felt a tremendous surge of attraction. "Why was it that she never met any strong and gentle types?" Confident they were the best, Shirley made a mental note to try to meet him when the flight terminated in Seattle.

The bold, attractive eyes of the flight attendant disturbed Saleem; the woman did not know her place. In his country, women never looked directly into a man's eyes, it was not proper. A strange, new feeling tingled through him, he could not help enjoy the way her eyes attracted him.

Unsettled, he leaned back in his seat, casually glancing at the sleeping woman across from him. Her serene face reminded him of his mother, a loving, gentle woman. Saleem remembered her tender affection for all things in the universe and her desire to please Allah. After his father's rages, she had been his refuge. His mother would wait until the storm was over and her husband would leave, only then, she would come to her son's aid. Saleem could still feel her taking him into the shelter of her arms, easing his bruises with ointments and the wounds in his heart with kisses. Whispering motherly love forever, she would hold him gently in her arms until he fell asleep. Laying his head back on the seat, he looked out of the airliner's oval window at the huge silver moon, the dark midnight sky filled with brilliant, sparkling stars, Saleem gently floated with the soft memories.

His thoughts began to drift to other memories. He recalled his friends, a secret group of extremists, their leader a soft-spoken patriarch. Very learned about the needs of Allah, the patriarch blurred the teachings of Saleem's mother to suit Saleem's anger. It had a huge appetite, feeding ravenously on the new ideas. Saleem remembered how the man helped him to achieve personal goals making his self-esteem grow. Saleem's anger began imitating the voice of his mother's Allah, feeding its own need, drifting Saleem slowly in its personal direction

Affection and loyalty for the patriarch increased until he began confiding and revealing the forbidden, his family life. The patriarch connected his father to simple corruption by wealth and power. He convinced Saleem his father was like an infidel and compared him to the Americans. He taught Saleem that rage is selfish and destructive, it does not recognize right or wrong, it only requires release for its personal closure. However anger when controlled, is like a sharp sword. Saleem's anger needed closure so he pointed him at America; it was the way.

His head resting against the seat cushion of the plane, Saleem looked through the airliner's window at the midnight sky. Memories slowly began their parade again; he remembered the beatings by his father, hot flames of anger flooded through his body. Then through the storm of anger, the patriarch's voice spoke to him, reminding him of his mission. Remembering the patriarch's kindness, strong loyalty rose in him like a light, pointing the way. Saleem knew it was his individual duty to help the secret group find the soft underbelly of America, the Great Satan.

Suddenly, Saleem could feel the sword of Allah in both his hands; America was the release for his anger. He would find the soft spot and rid a corrupt system full of people like his father, sacrifice a few to help many, the cost in a true purpose.

Saleem continued to look at the large, mystic moon, the midnight blue sky filled with tiny, sparkling diamonds; his need to cleanse America rose in him like a strong wind filling a sail, expanding his chest, tingling through his body.

Saleem Mohammad dal Figar closed his eyes; the ghostly, silver jetliner raced through midnight colored skies toward America and a destiny to come.

CHAPTER - 2

Spring in the Pacific Northwest of America is a spectacular mixture of pink, cherry blossoms and huge, fluffy, white clouds floating in the blue sky. The salty fragrance of the Pacific Ocean is everywhere.

Nestled on the rim of the Pacific Ocean, Seattle, Washington resembles a mirage. It is an extremely busy city, the hub of the state. Freeways leading in from the north, south and east resemble rivers of vehicles. Seagulls are everywhere and they are excited. They are excited about just being a seagull, gliding around the sky screaming this excitement to each other. Spring is the beginning of all things to come, particularly this spring.

Saleem Mohamed Dhal Figar slid open the glass door leading to the balcony of his hotel suite; he stepped out into a blend of beauty and traffic clamor. A blue, snow-capped mountain towered to his left; deserted by other mountain ranges, it stood alone. To the right, the sunlit glitter of the Pacific Ocean caught his eye. Saleem stood looking at the landscape and city. Traffic below him was churning out clamor that rose to lose itself among the soft, white clouds. Elation tingled within him; he had penetrated America without detection.

Saleem entered as a tourist, there was nothing to "red flag" the U.S. immigration officer on duty. He watched as the officer identified with his passport; it was proper and looked like thousands of others he examined daily. Seattle was a busy airport and the officer needed to move the people along, he looked away from Saleem, "Next." He said.

Saleem stepped onto American soil.

Now standing on the balcony of his hotel suite, pressure to fulfill his goal started to rise within Saleem. He must stay focused; Allah and his leader were depending on him, failure out of the question.

His aging father's burden of guilt made him agree to the prospects of starting a business in America; he arranged credit cards linked to the family business, promising large sums of money when required. Saleem felt no remorse to use his father's money, retribution for all the hurt to his mother and himself. His father should pay for his mistakes. Allah demanded this justice; Saleem's jihad had a camouflage.

A feeling to move forward came over Saleem. As he stood looking over the city and the ocean, the many tasks started to pressure him. A feeling to move forward came over him; he turned and walked back through the glass doors into the hotel.

His suite was luxurious, tastefully decorated to attract affluent, world travelers. None of the lavishness stirred Saleem; he was used to wealth and its addictions.

Quickly he showered and dressed in casual slacks and a short-sleeved shirt. The clothes were American style allowing him to blend into the environment. No one would notice a Middle Eastern man "dressed American" going about his business.

Saleem called down to the front desk and inquired about a car-rental. A soft female voice answered, it was very polite, softly purring the information to him, it seemed to Saleem she was almost enticing him. "American women were certainly bold." Again, something unfamiliar stirred within him.

The woman advised him a car rental agency had an arrangement with the hotel. A vehicle of his choice would be at the front entrance. Saleem ordered a BMW, his favourite and something familiar, the woman's soft, enticing voice informed him the car would be at the front entrance in an hour. The voice left him unsettled with the strange, new feeling he did not understand. Taking a deep breath, Saleem, opened the door of his suite, turned and walked toward the elevator, trying to focus on breakfast and his day.

Waiting for the elevator, the woman's voice tickled at Saleem's thoughts, he stood listening to it. A strange, new feeling kept trying to surface within him, something he had not experienced during his adolescence or manhood. It was a forbidden feeling, it had a delicious flavour, Saleem's instincts tried to fight but the flavour kept weakening him, growing stronger. Abruptly the elevator reached his floor, shattering the mood.

The elevator door slid open. It revealed an interior crowded with men; they all stood looking at him, their eyes bold and questioning, tightness rapidly spread through Saleem's body. Suddenly as if on a signal, they began opening their ranks allowing him space, some offered "Good morning." With extreme difficulty, Saleem returned the greeting, tension surging, growing. Saleem stood quietly, avoiding eye contact, struggling with the congestion in the elevator. Abruptly, the elevator stopped at another floor, its doors slid open to reveal an attractive blonde woman framed in the opening. She was young, pretty and extremely shapely, her dress revealing a great deal of woman. It exposed her neck, shoulders, her ample cleavage and long shapely legs. The woman had added high heels to accent her long, elegant legs. Curly, blonde hair framed her pretty face.

She stood looking into the crowded elevator filled with men, her large, blue eyes searching; everyone stood waiting in silence. The young woman's eyes found Saleem and appraised his good looks, their eyes met; he looked away, she made her decision instantly. The attractive, young woman stepped into the elevator and again the congestion of men separated for her, she entered, turned and stood directly in front of Saleem.

Saleem had never been this close to a woman dressed to reveal so much of her body. In his country, all women wore a hijab and a veil covered their face.

A man never saw anything but their hands and eyes. This attractive, blonde woman was an explosion to his senses. The first awareness he had was her perfume. Freshly showered, she had chosen an expensive fragrance to blend with her skin oils, the result erotic.

Saleem stood there, the intoxicating fragrance combined with the aroma of woman slowly invading his nostrils; he went adrift emotionally.

Struggling to cope with strange, new assault on his senses, he examined the back of her blonde head. Her hair styled to accent its natural curls, made little, sensual whisks around her delicate ears; it nestled on the back of her slender, elegant neck. His eyes traveled over the naked curves of her shoulders. The woman's erotic aroma was a flavour he would never forget, Saleem was changing, and he was powerless to stop it.

Abruptly the elevator stopped again, interrupting the moment.

An older man and woman stood in the doorway. They anxiously looked for space in the crowded elevator. Again, the spontaneous flow of movement to make room forced the blonde woman to step back, pressing gently against Saleem. Trapped, he could feel the firm curves of her buttocks gently pressing against him; the elevator resumed its journey.

The woman turned her head sideways, smiled and then shifted her hips. Saleem could feel her firm, buttocks roll against him. Trapped by this erotic assault, he was unaware America was slowly, steadily invading him.

With a slight bump, the elevator reached the lobby; its doors slid open again shattering his mood. Milling started, everyone trying to exit, taking his or her personal direction.

The young woman was gone, leaving Saleem struggling with his emotional disturbance. A voice gave him back control, "excuse me Sir, are you going up?" Saleem politely excused himself and stepped out into the lobby. Looking around for the front desk, a line of people gave him direction. Taking his place at the end of the line, he glanced around the elaborate lobby for the attractive woman, her fragrance and the sensation of her still lingering. He could feel a sense of emptiness, almost a sadness that took place, filling her space.

His anxious eyes finally found the blonde woman talking to a man. Abruptly, man took her by the arm, and as they turned, she looked around. Her large, blue eyes made contact with Saleem. She smiled the most radiant smile he had ever seen, and then allowed the man to lead her away. Saleem stood for long moments, totally lost in an emotional land he would never leave again.

The line of people waiting at the check-in counter slowly decreased and Saleem stepped up to the front desk. He began discussing his needs with a man behind the counter.

"Good morning, I am from room 2415. I requested an automobile delivered to the front entrance for me?"

The clerk checked his computer and looked up smiling. "Yes there has sir. They left the keys with the valet at the front entrance; you can pick the vehicle at your convenience."

"Please make all the necessary arrangements to charge everything to my room." Saleem instructed the clerk.

"No problem sir." The clerk confirmed the process. Saleem turned and walked away, instinctively glancing around for the blonde woman, she had left him in an emotional void; he felt abandoned.

CHAPTER – 3

Outside, at the entrance to the hotel, he found the valet, gave his name and shortly a dark grey BMW rolled up to the curb. The valet opened the driver's door for him and a smell of the new, leather interior gushed out. Saleem sat in the car and looked around, the familiar vehicle brought his objective into focus, energized he drove away from the hotel.

Directions memorized from a map in his hotel suite took him to a freeway leading north to a little town called Blaine, close to the Canadian border. In the yellow pages, he had found the name of a lawyer specializing in immigration.

His appointment was not until 2:00 p.m., giving Saleem a leisurely drive through the green, countryside. It was lush and beautiful, very different from the rolling sand hills of his home.

The interstate freeway led him slowly north passing small cities and farms. Saleem looked around enjoying the tranquil countryside. As he drove, flashbacks of his past again danced in his head.

His life had been the best and worst. He had known nothing other than addictive pleasure of money and bottomless anger from the pain his father had also provided.

The addictive, power of money had captured him, he rapidly learned from his father the ways to use it for manipulation. He heard his father brag how he had secured something of value by luring someone into his trap with a little wealth.

When the images of his father flashed, Saleem could feel the sharp edges of anger but now it gave his life meaning, he was a new person, a soldier for Allah, and this gave him immense pride and motivation.

While the sleek BMW raced along the freeway, his mind became free and open, it soared; suddenly, through this opening, the blonde woman entered, smiling at him. He could feel her softly touching him with her firm body; she had left him greatly troubled.

Shaking his head to regain control, he tried to focus on the serene hills pacing his car and purpose slowly came back. Leaning back, he could not understand why his thoughts were disobeying him; his body seemed to have a secret fire, simmering.

To regain control, Saleem glanced into the rear-view mirror; in the distance, he could see a white car following him. Red and blue lights were flashing on its roof; he watched the car rapidly catch up to him.

Instinctively he knew it was a police car, he could feel the muscles tighten in his stomach, his hands gripped the steering wheel. The police car pulled up behind the BMW and stayed there. Saleem could see the lone, police officer talking into the radio; it seemed the police officer was looking directly at him. "I am discovered." Suddenly the police car pulled beside his car, the officer looked over and touched two fingers to the brim of his hat in a salute. Saleem heard a sudden roar and the nose of the police car lifted, it accelerated, rapidly leaving him behind.

A feeling of appreciation for American friendliness started to grow; they were indeed soft and unsuspecting, easily fooled. Saleem realized it could be to his advantage, if he maintained appearances, things would go in his favour. Pleased, he leaned over and dropped his left elbow onto the armrest of the car.

He gripped the steering wheel more firmly with his right hand and drove on with increased confidence.

The little town of Blaine sat just back from the border crossing into Canada. It had basic services, gas stations, small markets and a few restaurants. The lawyer's office was on the second floor of an old brick building. It showed only moderate signs of success. Saleem mentally noted that money could be a useful advantage here

Dennis Hall attorney-at-law was bald and portly, over time, his practice had grown and so had his body. Trying to radiate friendship and trust, he almost came over the top of his desk to shake Saleem's hand, the handshake been developed over many years to relax his clients. His smile and demeanour were warm but his eyes were predatorial. Dennis had been a lawyer for many years and had developed hunting instincts.

After the basic formalities, Dennis began to probe for his revenue. After all, clients with no money were just part of the world's problems and Dennis had resigned as General Manager of the Universe a long time ago. His questions were calculated probes, searching and searching for the eternal motivator, money.

Saleem sat looking at this American lawyer and saw his father; the man was aggressive and greedy. He could feel the probes; soft but obvious, money kept rising to the surface. He knew his next move and sat allowing the lawyer to manipulate him.

When he felt an opening, Saleem shrewdly revealed that he was part of a business plan for a Middle Eastern oil tycoon who wanted to expand into North America.

Feeling the sudden rush of information he had been seeking, Dennis leaned back into his black, leather chair. As they talked, Dennis would constantly try maintaining eye contact with Saleem. Saleem would confirm his intentions were genuine with direct eye contact with the other man's eyes. It was a war; Saleem knew he could win.

Dennis could feel a strong excitement building, pressure rising within him; he had never worked with an extremely rich client. Many had been Asians and they had enough capital to afford consulting him and to purchase a business, they could not compare with this bottomless oil well.

"Yes we can establish you in North America by obtaining a green card, but it's going to take serious money." Dennis said. A good probe and not a soft one, it cut right to the chase, he watched Saleem intently.

Aware, Saleem again allowed their eyes to meet. "That will not be a problem." He fed the man's greed; the man across from him followed the trail of morsels

Excited, growing more confident, Dennis continued. "All US immigration wants to hear are three things, one is that you are bringing money, two is that your company will create jobs and three is the fact that only you personally can run the company in this country." Dennis took a deep breath, hoping it would not be noticeable. Saleem again looked directly at the lawyer assuring him that a large retainer would be available.

A sudden energy pushed Dennis forward in his chair; he could feel his chest expanding, his shoulders growing tighter. The man across from him had taken all the probes with sincerity, confidence surged through him.

"There will be searches by the FBI through for anything that is not proper. Once all the information is gathered and approved, we can then talk about structuring your business and easing you through all the red tape in this country. Before we continue, a retainer will be necessary." He searched Saleem's face for positive confirmation.

Saleem sat across from the lawyer and began closing the trap; he looked directly into the man's greedy, glowing eyes and nodded his head.

"$10,000.00 US can be delivered immediately; it will be a gesture of good faith. Even if not all goes well with the FBI investigation, you may keep the money. We would like to start off properly with you." Saleem snapped the trap shut by looking directly into the lawyer's expectant eyes.

Dennis could not believe his ears, today this was a bigger game than he had ever been in. He had established many immigrants over the years. All had been coming to the United States to start fresh. He obtained a visa for them and never saw them again, but this was very different. His mind raced with the prospects of oil money pouring his way, he smiled at Saleem envisioning endless retainers. Dennis saw a cash flow that only happened once in a lifetime. All his years in practice had honed his negotiation skills to perfection; Dennis did not betray his explosive excitement, he leaned back in his black, leather chair; he had won the money game. Saleem closed by saying, "$10,000.00 will be fine for now.

Dennis continued with closure, "Please leave me a number where you can be reached and once I receive your retainer, the necessary action can be taken."

Glancing at the lawyer's eyes Saleem saw the movement, a slight shift, a shadow passing in the man's mind. The same would happen with his father, Saleem had learned well.

Taking the lawyer's hand, Saleem smiled, knowing precisely what he had purchased. A steady flow of money and this greedy infidel would work hard to provide him with necessary camouflage.

After providing the lawyer with all the necessary details, Saleem walked out into a beautiful day. The air was moist with a fragrance of growing things. It was beautiful in America, truly like an Oasis.

His jihad was beginning to take shape. Excitement pushing him, Saleem took the entrance to the freeway that lead south and Seattle.

The sun had dropped lower over the western ocean. Golden light and soft shadows blended to make a beautiful pacific coast evening.

Settling into the comfortable leather seat of the BMW, Saleem watched the freeway slide endlessly beneath the car taking him deeper into the soft heart of America.

CHAPTER – 4

It was Friday and Carla Black sat at her desk shuffling papers. Her computer tinkled a reminder about her 3:00 p.m. appointment, the client was Saleem dal Figar. She looked at the name; it raised no curiosity so she continued with the paper shuffle.

Carla Black is an attractive woman; rich auburn hair compliments her eyes that are so green they startle you. An above average taste for style constantly enhances her good looks. The position as manager of foreign accounts with a multinational, U.S. bank provides a good income allowing her to enjoy a late model sports car and comfortable apartment in an upscale part of Seattle. Carla loves fine dining, dancing and good music, a woman full of energy; she needs the pace of the world.

Carla Black is alone her weekends are full of desolation and loneliness, the only escape is Monday and her work that are a light in the distance.

Carla's marriage traveled a full circle; she entered the circle to join hands with a controlling and abusive husband, a sentence that lasted four years. Fortunately, before her spirit broke one morning during a hot shower, a place for all good ideas, Carla suddenly knew it was over. When the solution to her bad marriage hit, it was as if a great weight was suddenly gone. She stood in the shower feeling the flow of release. Carla Black suddenly understood that the physical and verbal abuse was a barrier in her marriage she could never go over or around, it was finished. There was no sadness or remorse, Carla left for work that morning and never went back.

In his dark rage over losing control, her husband threatened to destroy Carla and her job. There were many other cruel things before the divorce; he worked hard to build the final, ultimate barrier between them. When his rages and threats proved futile, he changed his tactics and became repulsive. He began telling her how much he loved and needed her. In the end, her husband did an excellent job convincing Carla that she made a wise decision to get rid of him. That had been the easy part.

When their marital storm and divorce were over, the loneliness became so deep and dark for Carla that she entered the singles world. It was full of male predators, who all wanted just her body. She made fatal mistakes in the beginning, taking some good-looking men home, bad decision.

All had the same selfish motives and wanted the same thing. Some wanted it before dinner; some after dinner and others could have during dinner. How do you get rid of a man who has not yet appeased his personal hunger for a woman? If they had too much to drink, it is tedious, it they are sober it is difficult, sometimes hazardous. You can ask them to leave but they will negotiate, the harder they try, the more disenchanting it becomes. It left her puzzled why men just never understand the many flavors of love. She exited the sad and misguided singles world; it left her jaded and cynical. Starting with her husband, she had begun to dislike just about all kinds of men. Her pride and mistrust would not allow her to place herself in another compromising situation.

At the end of the day, another bleak and lonely weekend waited for her like a cage. She could feel depression slowly easing its shadow over her. It felt like the sun sliding behind a cloud taking its warmth and comfort away.

Today was Friday with no place to go but her empty apartment.

Shortly past lunch, Carla slowly worked at her desk, waiting for the appointment; it was her last for the day. She slowly completed paperwork that would give her an easier Monday. Suddenly she sensed something; she looked up and saw a co-worker, Jerry Worsley standing in the doorway of her office. He had been watching her, Jerry stood leaning against the doorway with a half-smile on his face, unable to hide the truth behind his eyes.

"How are things Carla?" Jerry broke the uneasy silence between them.

Carla could feel her spine stiffening rapidly, claws of pressure grabbing her shoulders. She had mistakenly slept with Jerry on one occasion and he had left her soiled and angry. Naively, she had given him her body, tenderness, and affection; he had left it all like a trampled flower. Carla swore she would never humiliate herself in that fashion ever again.

Using forced, professional civility, she said, "Just finishing before the weekend."

A tremble started in her back, rapidly migrating to her hands.

"Home alone, again this weekend?" Jerry asked, walking slightly into her office and leaning back against the wall. A decent looking man, he had black hair, pale blue eyes, medium height, and build, a proper masculine package. It was the content of that package; it was not a secret anymore; Jerry had revealed all to Carla. She struggled to keep the disgust and coldness from her voice, "I have plans."

"Come on Carla, what plans? Watching TV all weekend?" Jerry sneered. We could have dinner tonight and then see what develops." With hungry eyes, he stood there leaning against the wall.

Carla pressed her trembling hands hard on the desk and forced herself to look down at her work. The man totally sickened her; she did not dare look up at him. "I have plans, and I have a 3:00 p.m. appointment coming." She said, fighting to hide the tremble that had migrated to her voice. Then suddenly like a gust of wind, her steel resolve came to her rescue, it was time to end it. Carla looked up; Jerry was still leaning against the wall looking at her with hungry eyes.

"Come on Carla, what is it with you?" I'm offering a night out."

To Carla it sounded like she should grovel in appreciation.

"I told you Jerry, but I have plans." Carla's voice was now hostile and frigid, "And now if you will excuse me, but I have to prepare for my appointment."

He stood looking at her for what seemed eternity, suddenly he sneered, "Whatever." Worsley turned and stomped out of her office, Carla watched him rapidly walk away.

Her hatred for the man was deepening from the constant confrontations.

Slowly resuming her work, Carla struggled to relax deeper, time passed and her three o'clock was almost due. She stood up and went to get a drink of water.

Standing beside the office water cooler, sipping cold water, she had a feeling of sadness come over her. Carla felt stranded and alone, her day was dissolving rapidly leaving her a weekend she could not face. Finishing the water, glancing at her watch, she slowly, sadly walked back to her desk.

There was a knock on her door, a well-dressed, good-looking man stood in the doorway. "You must be Saleem dal Figar," she asked. "Yes I am," the man confirmed. "Please come in and have a seat," Carla gestured to the two chairs in front of her desk.

Saleem saw her glance shift from a direct look. Instantly he looked more closely at the woman. She was pretty but did not dress to reveal herself; the woman seemed to know her place. "America has some good women." He mused secretly.

Carla looked up from her desk and smiled at Saleem, she searched his face avoiding direct eye contact with his large, brown, liquid eyes. He had a thin, white scar running down his cheek. "How interesting, a man of mystery," she thought.

Carla took in the handsome, masculine appeal of the man sitting across from her. His clothes were casual, but chosen with good taste. He had an expensive watch on his wrist, an elaborate gold ring on a finger of his right hand. Feminine instinct took her eyes to his left hand there were no rings. Their eyes collided, this time the man across from her looked away, Carla felt her heart skip a beat. Taking a deep breath, she stiffened her back and her resolve. One thing she did not need in her life was a man.

"How may I help you?" She said softly, looking down demurely at the papers on her desk.

"We are planning offices in Seattle and require a bank account." Saleem informed Carla.

The magnetism between them receded as Carla focused on the necessary forms. When Saleem leaned over to sign, a subtle fragrance of expensive men's cologne teased at Carla, triggering another surge of feminine attraction. Annoyed with herself for noticing all the enticing features of this man, she struggled harder with her resolve.

When all was completed, Saleem stood up and offered his hand, Carla stood up accepting his handshake. She could not help noticing that it was a gentle grip, respectful of a woman's hand. Before Carla could remove her hand, she felt a tingle pass between her and the man.

When Saleem took the cool, soft hand of the woman, she smiled at him then looked away. "What an elegant woman" he thought.

Carla leaned over and took her business card from a holder on her desk. "Please call me in a couple of days," she stated. "I will have all the final paperwork for you to endorse."

"Thank you, I will call." Saleem confirmed. Also I would like to thank for being so helpful, it is sincerely appreciated."

She struggled not to look directly into his eyes even though they were deep, dark pools of mystery.

Saleem turned and walked out of her office, Carla looked up and could not stop herself from noticing his solid shoulders and trim hips. He dressed tastefully and walked with a good masculine movement. A sensation of pleasure passed through her, she struggled for self-control, looking away from the retreating man.

"What is happening to me," she thought?

Saleem walked out of the bank to his waiting BMW. His thoughts were still on the attractive woman. She certainly knew how to be feminine and know her place; he liked her looks and her ways.

"These are the kind of people my jihad will help. It will change their lives by freeing them from the corruption that exists in America" he reaffirmed as he walked to his car.

Carla sat at her desk and could not close out the excitement she felt; it showed up in her heart. It was beating rapidly and there was a slight tremor in her hand. She had not felt this way since she was a young girl. She looked up again to see if Saleem had actually gone and when she could not see him, a feeling of disappointment passed through her.

Slowly Carla started shuffling papers around trying to focus and prepare for the bleak weekend waiting to close around her.

CHAPTER − 5

The setting sun touched the tips of the mountains, giving the blankets of snow a ruby hue, darkening the sky into the deep blue that forms the end of a glorious day. Dark shadows were forming on the mountains giving them more texture by darkening the green forests covering them. The first star twinkled; it was a peaceful and tranquil scene.

Neil Chambers and his wife Ellen drove through this majesty of nature in a spiritual silence. They were a close couple blessed with love, the very elusive bond. A similar taste for nature such as the grandeur of the coastal mountains, made the decision spontaneous to drive from Seattle to San Diego on their annual vacation. Now, they were going home after enjoying a mutual pleasure, the San Diego Zoo.

The vacation and evening were ending in grandeur.

Neil Chambers was an FBI agent; he worked with the Special Counter-Terrorism Unit in Seattle. A very intense quiet man with a driven integrity for his job, he could not and would not rest until he found missing pieces and created justice. He had a quirk that annoyed co-workers. During a conversation, he became silent and looked away into the distance. During this silence, he entered his special emotional place and mentally sorted all the tiny pieces of information. Because of this special focus, Neil was good at his job. Crowned with copper colored hair, Neil was not handsome, just average but looks are deceiving, Neil was not average, he loved his wife and had total devotion for his job.

Ellen Chambers a petite, dark-haired woman, had eyes that sparkled and were constantly restless, her sensitivity a deep river. Today she sat and looked out of the cars' window; her soul was full to the brim with contentment. Turning her head slightly, she saw the tiny, brilliant, evening star, she looked at the sunset coloring the mountains, and then she looked at her husband. The afterglow of the day blended with her love for her him; it flowed through her like a strong current. Her world was so beautiful that she decided she would live forever.

Clinging to the side of the mountain, the winding road curved left. A huge, black truck came roaring around the curve, it was on the wrong side of the road. Chrome exhaust stacks suddenly spurted black smoke; the truck driver began fighting for control.

Neil Chambers and his wife Ellen could hear the loud blasts from the truck's air horn and the angry roaring of the engine. For microseconds, Neil froze, and then suddenly a powerful rush rose in him. He spun the steering wheel to the right trying to avoid the huge, black, monster truck rushing directly at them. Stomping the accelerator to the floor, he could feel the car surge with power. It was too late.

If Neil and Ellen had taken seconds from anywhere in their lives to love a bit longer, to hold hands longer or just enjoy each other longer, it would have robbed this tragedy of its explosive sequence. These stolen seconds would have allowed Neil to swerve aside missing the truck.

Today, these seconds were destiny.

Fighting to avoid the wall of steel roaring down on them, Neil angled the car across the highway into a fatal position. The huge truck's massive, chrome and steel bumper smashed into the car's rear fender exploding the tire. The terrible force distorted the entire shape of the car forcing the rear window to burst outwards. Little pieces of glass fell sparkling like diamonds in the fading, afternoon sunlight. The black truck and its huge trailer roared past. Neil's foot still jammed down onto the accelerator, forced the car to leap for the edge of the road where a deadly drop waited. Out of control, the car leaped off the side of the mountain, taking flight to its final resting place.

All violence of the crash seemed in slow motion, offering Neil a few more minutes of precious reflection. He watched the landscape whirl by his windshield, wondering if this was his last ride. Suddenly he wished desperately he could live to love again.

Neil knew he must protect his wife from harm at all costs. He reached out with his arm and placed it in front of Ellen. "I love you!" he shouted. Fate allowed him only this short passionate statement.

Gravity beckoned from below, forcing the car to lose its flight path. Slowly, like a tired arrow, its nose began dropping, its energy spent; the battered automobile began its fatal fall.

A huge, gray boulder lurked, waiting in the brush on the mountain slope. The car struck the boulder nose first; the impact crushed the front of the vehicle. Slowly the car began to turn over on its roof breaking brush and small trees that had hidden the huge boulder. Good fortune was a passenger in the car this black day. Trees and shrubs concealing the boulder, helped to soften and cushion the car's fall, protecting Neil from the killing force.

In the midst of the sound of cracking trees, breaking glass, screeching metal, Ellen could not stop screaming. Then as the car rested for a moment on the brush of the mountainside, she felt the strength of Neil's arm protecting her, the warmth of the feeling stayed with Ellen until her end came.

For the time of a few heartbeats, there was silence, gravity was insistent. With a crackle of breaking branches and the groan of its tortured metal body, the car rolled over and resumed its journey. It started to cartwheel end for end, crashing down the side of the mountain. A large tree had died and fallen on this lonely mountainside. Hardening in the sun, wind, and rain for hundreds of years, it waited for Ellen and this day of horror.

The dead tree held a broken limb out like a spear.

In its throes of death, the car rolled onto the dead tree. Hard as steel and needle sharp, the long, gray limb came through the empty space where the car's windshield had been, it entered Ellen's chest, and the pain was like an explosion.

For a moment, there was silence on the mountain, and then with a groan of metal, the car slowly rolled off the tree, pulling the gray, bloodied spear from Ellen's chest. Gently the car continued to roll down the rock-strewn slope, crushing shrubs and rolling over boulders, finally coming to rest on the ground far below the highway.

Ellen was still living, hanging upside down in her seat belt. The silence was overwhelming. She could hear the pinging of metal and an occasional groan from the carcass of the wrecked car. As the silence deepened, slowly and painfully, Ellen turned her head to look at Neil, he was not moving. Sadness flooded through her and she raised her arm with great difficulty and placed her hand tenderly on Neil's bloodied face in a final farewell. Her last page ended, and her book of life closed, her soul left her body like teardrops.

A distant voice kept repeating a name gently; it seemed like a memory, trying to find its way back. The voice kept calling softly, gently, trying to persuade him to follow; he could not seem to find the familiar name in his memory.

"Neil." The gentle voice coaxed. He decided to follow and see who belonged to the voice. As he struggled through the mists, unexpectedly there was a distant light. He forced himself toward the light. Slowly the light became a window with sunlight streaming in, bathing the wall beside his bed. Focusing on the window, he saw blue sky and sunlight and suddenly he knew the name. It was his name, it was Sunday and a beautiful day. Ellen was calling him for breakfast.

Bracing to rise and meet the day, the pain became so sudden and intense it made him gasp. "Neil, please don't move. You have been badly injured!" He looked around for Ellen because he could not understand why her voice was so different. It was a young woman, not Ellen. Panic started to rise, taking him where the pain was waiting.

"Who are you?" The exertion to speak made his chest hurt. "Where is Ellen?" he said, bracing for the pain, a throbbing pain in his head, squeezing, blurring his vision.

"You have been in a serious car accident. You are in a hospital." The young woman informed him.

"Who are you, where is my wife?" The pain had many sharp cutting edges.

"I am going to give you something for the pain. We will talk later." He felt the young woman take his arm from under the blanket. He felt the sharp prick of a needle, the sudden, golden flow through his body made everything seem distant and unimportant.

Saleem dal Figar was back in his hotel suite in Seattle. Turning on the television, he watched local news. Since his arrival in America, he was pleased with the progress of his jihad. His thoughts drifted to the blonde woman in the elevator, He remembered the scent of her perfume, the fragrance of a woman. He could feel the contours of her body against him, the flashbacks again left him disturbed and unsettled.

Abruptly, a news flash on TV interrupted his mental travel. An FBI agent from the Special Terrorism Unit was badly injured and his wife killed. They were returning from a vacation, driving through the mountains from San Diego to Seattle. A spokesperson from the bureau said they both enjoyed mountain scenery and had chosen to drive instead of flying. Emergency medical personnel had airlifted Neil Chambers to a Seattle hospital.

Saleem knew about the FBI and now there would be one less infidel watching him. Glancing at his Rolex watch, Saleem realized it was late. The next day would be busy for him.

He lay in bed looking at the indistinct shadows in his suite. The pleasure of his connection with Allah seemed eroded by the blonde woman in the elevator and the attractive woman at the bank, Saleem drifted into a troubled sleep.

CHAPTER – 6

Hamid al-Issa was furious; they had betrayed him.

To escape a difficult life as a police officer in the Middle East, he moved his family to Seattle, desperate to experience the American Dream. Employed as a security guard in a high-rise, office tower, he worked hard, but the wages allowed only a modest apartment in a less desirable part of a city.

At his work, there had been talk about a promotion to supervisor; the increase in wages could be substantial. He lay awake some nights and visualized a house, a better car, and a comfortable lifestyle. Could the American Dream be within his grasp?

This morning, Hamid al-Issa arrived at work very excited. The notice on the lunchroom bulletin board shattered that dream. All his hard work, wasted on their blind eyes, they had chosen a lazy co-worker to be the new supervisor. They seemed to favor their own; it left him with a bitter taste of defeat.

A tickle of guilt probed at his anger, he remembered speaking out about America and its attitudes. He pushed it out of his mind; they were blind and did not understand the truth. Hamid went through half his shift feeling lost and helpless, brooding over the injustice. He had nowhere to turn. His pride as a man, would not allow him to confide in his wife, it would be humiliation. Hamid was hurt and alone.

During his routine duties, Hamid entered his memories, they took him home to the Middle East, and he remembered some happy times. Suddenly his missed his homeland, friends, and family. His missed the food, the way of life and the good times. Sadness flowed through him. He sat looking at his now tasteless lunch, questioning his motives about coming to America. Maybe it had not been so bad back home. Images of his best friends flashed into his mind, warm memories of their talks, the plans they had made for better futures. Dismally he looked up and around the lunchroom. Hamid al-Issa wondered if he had made a very bad decision by coming to America. Brooding through his lunch break, he struggled with his thoughts, making a half-hearted attempt to finish his now tasteless food.

Hatred rose in him like a sudden wind. The American Dream was a lie.

Clenching his fists, Hamid al-Issa struggled with the river of emotion until his anger suddenly spoke to him. Hurt them back for causing him pain; give them a taste of pain and humiliation. Hamid's anger searched for answers. Could he perform a secret jihad that would teach them a lesson and rescue his pride? Could he hurt his employers while he looked for work elsewhere? No one would know.

Sorting through his past, he recalled a group back in his homeland that had tried to recruit him to be a soldier for Allah. They wanted him to perform terrorist acts from inside the police department, but the idea had worried him, it offered no money and risked his position at the police department. If something went wrong, how would his wife and child live while he was being a soldier for Allah? At that time, his reasoning had seemed very good.

Hamid's thoughts swirled, ideas hurtling into his mind, he still had the leader's telephone number, and he needed help. He did not know anything about secret jihads, only that they required skillful planning. Hamid rose suddenly from the luncheon table to work his plan. Tonight he would telephone his homeland.

The leader of the group, pleased to hear from him, listening quietly while Hamid vented about the injustice done to him in America.

"That is the American way, they are corrupt and evil," the leader, agreed. "We will be pleased to help you teach them a lesson. I will put you in touch with someone who is in America now, and he is one of us."

Waiting for contact, the days passed slowly, Hamid's job became more unbearable. The new supervisor, corrupted by power, became a tyrant. He now bullied people he had disliked in the past. He singled Hamid out often, knowing he had wanted the position. Daily, the supervisor took pride in humiliating him, until anger and resentment grew in Hamid like a fire out of control.

Emotionally, he reached a point of no return and could no longer go back on his plan. Punishing his employers for unleashing this weak infidel would be just and right. Often he would go to bed early, going over the plan in his mind until he could not seem to wait for the next day. He would finally fall asleep to have wild dreams of a jihad.

The telephone call came when he least expected, the voice confident. "I am Saleem Mohammed dal Figar. I have been informed you are interested in becoming a soldier for Allah."

An old ghost of fear rose in Hamid. He became defensive, avoiding direct questions. As a police officer, he had learned quickly secrecy was a valuable trait; it was the way to avoid trouble with his superiors.

The conversation shifted to life in the Middle East, the memories slightly lowering the wall of Hamid's defense. The confident, male voice did most of the talking, drawing Hamid into the conversation. Finally, he accepted the man's suggestion to meet and talk more, Hamid revealed his address. After hanging up the telephone, another sudden attack of anxiety surged through him, he began to wonder if he was doing the right thing. Deep in thought, Hamid stood for a long time looking out of the window.

Saleem called down to the front desk, requesting the valet to bring his car to the main entrance of the hotel. When he stepped out of the elevator, the lobby was a beehive of activity, and luggage lay piled near the front desk, a long line of people stood waiting.

Avoiding the milling people, he rapidly walked toward the front door of the hotel, his car stood waiting at the curb. The valet caught his eye, smiled, extending his hand, it held a set of keys. Saleem tipped the man and got into his car. Consulting a map of the city, he found the area and street Hamid had revealed earlier. He pulled away from the curb skillfully easing his car into the river of other vehicles.

Weaving through the congestion of unskilled, Saturday morning drivers, Saleem mentally worked the telephone conversation with Hamid. The man had been very evasive and noncommittal, reluctantly agreeing to a meeting, selecting Saturday morning; it was his day off from work. As Saleem drove, something about the contact's evasive attitude kept disturbing him, caution would be the only way to operate.

The downtown area of Seattle gave way to residential housing, then gradually to an older part of the city. As he drove, the evidence of poverty became more visible. Litter on the front lawns, fences decayed, falling down. Houses gave way to apartment complexes, also old and poorly maintained. The littered sundecks had rusting gas barbecues, broken, plastic patio furniture, relics of better times. Driving slowly, Saleem looked around at the tired neighborhoods, deciding that in America not everyone was living the dream.

Hamid restlessly paced from room to room, trying to escape the increasing pressure of anxiety. His wife had gently asked him what was wrong. He did not answer. She quietly did her chores, glancing at him when she thought he was not looking.

To relieve some pressure, Hamid walked to the front window of his apartment and looked out. The early morning children were already playing on the street, and people were stirring about, everything seemed normal. Suddenly there was something different. He saw a dark grey, expensive, car moving slowly down his street. Warily, he watched the car drift along until it was across from his apartment building. Abruptly, it pulled over to the sidewalk and stopped. For what seemed eternity, nothing happened, then slowly the driver's door opened, man got out, stepped onto the sidewalk, and looked around. As if knowing the exact window where Hamid stood, he looked up and their eyes met, Hamid felt a sudden surge of bursting pressure in his chest. He noticed the man's dark hair and skin tone; it was someone from his homeland. The man turned and walked to the front entrance of the apartment building, the buzz of the intercom sounded.

"Is there anyone there named Hamid?" the metallic voice asked. "Who is asking?" Hamid asked warily. "This is Saleem Mohammed dal Figar; I am looking for Hamid al-Issa." His breath rapid and shallow, Hamid answered, "I will be right down!" Moving rapidly, he grabbed his jacket from the closet beside the front door. He left rapidly, slamming the door of their apartment behind him.

Roya saw her husband disappear into the hallway then she heard the hard sound of the door closing, instinctively she knew something was wrong, softly she murmured a prayer for her husband.

Hamid saw the grey BMW parked beside the curb, a man leaning back against it. The man leaned forward, walking toward Hamid with his right arm held out. "Are you Hamid al-Issa? I am Saleem Mohammed dal Figar."

The recent emotional bruising Hamid had taken in American made him vulnerable, lonely for his homeland. Instinctively he reached for Saleem's right hand, placing his left hand on the stranger's shoulder; he leaned over mimicking a kiss on both cheeks.

Turning, both men walked toward the car. Saleem opened the passenger's door, Hamid hesitated, then he leaned over and looked around the rich interior of the automobile, finally he got in, sitting in the expensive, leather seat and breathing in the new vehicle smell. He had never been inside a new BMW in his life. The wages of a police officer did not allow for such luxuries. His enjoyment abruptly interrupted when Saleem opened the driver's door and slid in behind the steering wheel.

A flow of pleasure passed through Hamid, he could feel the power as the car pulled away from the curb. He sat breathing in the fragrance of the car's leather interior, watching the street flow toward him.

"I have been told that you are interested in becoming a soldier for Allah." Saleem asked.

"I don't know." Hamid lapsed back into silence after his answer, his thoughts racing. His emotional handshake had not bonded him to a man who obviously, was rich and could afford the luxuries of pursing his convictions. He did not know the heavy weight of poverty, having to earn a living, a family to support. There was distance between him and this stranger. The tightness of fear and anxiety was a barrier. He sat in silence, watching the poor neighborhood flow past the car, noticing the neglected houses, old cars sitting in front of them. Sitting in the rich leather of the expensive car, Hamid felt trapped by his heavy burden of thoughts.

Saleem worked his car into the traffic flow, sensitive to the other man's silence. Glancing occasionally, he could see Hamid looking out the side window. Doubt trickled through Saleem's mind. Was this man sincere? Maybe he was a spy and a betrayer. Quickly looking back at the street and the traffic, Saleem became silent. He could not help noticing the neglected neighborhood, poverty everywhere. Suddenly he remembered the apartment building where Hamid lived. Maybe there was a way.

"Do you like this neighborhood?" he asked Hamid. For a moment, Hamid did not speak. As Saleem watched the flow of cars, he heard a soft sigh. "Would you?" Hamid asked.

The silence was back and Saleem glanced at the man again. He was looking out of the side window of the car again.

"Is there not enough pay from your work to allow you to move to a better place?" Saleem gently probed.

This time the silence was so long, Saleem thought Hamid would not answer such a question with its deep intrusion into a man's pride. He glanced at

Hamid, but the man was looking out of the window; the silence between them was thick.

Suddenly Hamid spoke, "There could have been enough pay!" The Americans preach their dream, but maybe it is only for them!" Saleem could feel the anger in the man's voice.

"Maybe it is a lie about becoming wealthy in America." Hamid spoke, bitter lines deepening around his mouth.

Saleem could sense anger rising within the man next to him, he had created an opening, and Hamid's feelings were beginning to flow out. He sat waiting for more to come, but suddenly there was silence again. Saleem glanced over and saw the man looking out of the window again. He drove on and waited.

"I have worked hard at the job, never missing work but when a promotion came up, they picked one of their own! The man is lazy, not even capable of looking after goats." Hamid's anger began rising, tension gripping his chest, and clawing at his shoulders.

"They are liars, all of them," tasting the bile of his anger. The recent abuse he had endured from the new supervisor made his emotional wounds very sensitive.

"What if there was a way you could get your revenge?" Saleem probed softly.

"I have thought about it. A hard earned job will be lost if they find out. That is the way in America; one requires references to get another job. They have a system here that protects them." Hamid's anger kept his voice loud.

Saleem knew he had pressed the right button.

"Would money help you and your family while you are searching for another job?" He continued probing. Saleem could sense that Hamid was looking at him. He glanced over and saw Hamid's eyes were wide and questioning. He kept feeding the financial carrot, "What if I could arrange money for you?

What if I could provide you with the best references assuring that you get hired?"

Hamid could not believe his ears, lies, betrayal, and politics were constant traps waiting for the unwary victim, and no one would trick him.

Noticing a park on his left, Saleem saw it was green and serene. They were out of the area of social decay. Pulling over to the curb, he shut off the car. Opening the door, he said. "Come, let us walk, and talk."

Walking across the street toward the park, he did not look back to see if Hamid was coming. When he heard the car door slam shut, he knew the man was following; money historically was the tool of choice

Saleem heard Hamid catch up to him. They walked in silence until Hamid could bear it no longer. "How do I know if this can be true?" He said, puffing with the exertion of catching up with Saleem.

"Allah unites you and me in a just cause, but Allah does not provide food and a place to live. I can do that for you if you help me punish the Americans." Saleem did not look at Hamid; he just kept walking through the green American oasis. The trees were showing new, bright leaves and the grass was soft underfoot. When he thought of the harsh heat, sand and the few soft green areas back home, he could not stop the feeling he was getting for America. He could sense the man walking behind in silence.

The exertion of walking and the excitement built up until Hamid could not contain his silence any longer. "Let us talk more!" he spoke in a gasp.

They had reached a bench for people to sit and enjoy the park. Saleem sat on the bench, and then he looked up at Hamid for approval, Hamid stood for a moment, deep in thought, then he sat on the bench.

"I am new in America and need soldiers, people like you to help me show the Americans how vulnerable they are. Together we can target their soft spots and hurt them. If you help, there could be money for you so that you and your family can be comfortable. The money should convince you that I am honorable and would not use or betray you!" Saleem laid out the key to the man's trust.

It was indeed the key; Hamid could not believe his ears. He could feel his heart beating against his ribs; he clenched his hands into fists.

A new job would make all things possible.

Hamid locked his eyes with Saleem's, "If you could do these things, we can start making plans." He said.

That night, Hamid lay in bed beside his sleeping wife, pleased with the control he now had over his life. Through the thin wall of the apartment, he could hear a baby crying, a woman's voice softly crooning to the child.

"Things will be better, he thought. I will teach them a lesson, get a better job with more pay and recognition, the house, and a nice car are still possible."

Next door, the baby had stopped crying and the mother's soothing voice, gently eased Hamid into sleep filled with dreams of a holy jihad.

CHAPTER − 7

The tiny, orange flame of the candle dominated the darkness with the arrogance of the first star of evening that captures the deep blue of the twilight sky. Celebrating its birth, the tiny flame danced with the shadows on the walls. It sat surrounded by oil soaked rags that formed a continuous trail leading off into the darkness.

Swaying and flickering, the excited, little flame voraciously ate the white wax of the candle, focused to reach the rags on the floor, there lay power. Once it reached the rags, it would have a path to glory. Impatiently the flame danced as it consumed the candle, clear wax flowing down the sides.

The office tower was majestic; its tinted glass windows mirrored the sun, making it resemble a black diamond pillar reaching up into the clear, blue, morning sky. Distanced from the others, it stood alone, posturing in elegance. The front entrance sat back under the tall building, creating a courtyard where service vehicles could park. Concrete supports held up the front part of the building. A small garden of flowers and shrubs separated the entrance from the street. The office tower was a jewel of downtown Seattle.

A white, mid-size, truck sat in the courtyard, directly under the building. Parked close to the front three pillars supporting the structure, the white truck had no distinctive markings. Service vehicles were common; it did not attract any special attention.

There was a security guard at his desk in the lobby of the building. He was reading the morning newspaper. Occasionally, he looked up and glanced around, wondering why he had not seen the truck arrive.

It was a pristine morning, the sky a pure, delicate blue, a Seattle fragrance in the air, the salty Pacific Ocean. Traffic had not reached the midmorning frenzy. Slowly, the city was awakening to another beautiful spring day in the Pacific Northwest.

A courier van drove up and parked behind the white truck. The driver got out and walked to the rear of his vehicle. Opening the doors, he selected a package then began walking toward the glass entrance of the office tower. The security guard looked up from the newspaper he was reading, he saw the uniformed, driver opening the glass doors of the office tower. He did not see the courier van parked behind the white truck; he assumed this was the missing driver. When the courier driver presented his waybill for the company listed on it, the security guard directed him to the correct floor. Pressure of concern reduced, the guard resumed reading his newspaper.

The tiny orange flame had eaten the white candle; it had reached the diesel soaked rags. Hesitating, the little flame flickered and danced with uncertainty, then with a "whoosh" it took its power, the tiny flame changed into a snake of fire. Its crimson flames leaped higher to reveal a dark doorway, the trail of rags enticing it to enter.

Racing along the rag trail, the snake of fire sped for the doorway. Rapidly growing in size, its flames gave more light, more definition to its prison, shadows danced on the walls. The snake of fire reached the doorway and entered. Again, for a moment it hesitated, studying the black mass of material piled almost to the ceiling. With a sudden surge, it struck at the black mass of mixed fertilizer and diesel oil, taking its final power.

The security guard saw a flash of light on his newspaper, heard the roar of the explosion. During the last microsecond of his life, he was unable to understand what was happening, he died instantly. Massive force of the explosion took the glass entrance and the security guard and turned all into a mist. Destiny brought a man down in the elevator opposite to the main entrance. When the elevator door opened, the man became part of the mist when the blast from hell entered the elevator. Acting like a gun barrel, the elevator shaft took the elevator like a bullet shooting to the roof and through it.

Outside the building, the explosive force looked everywhere for another weak spot to enter and destroy, Mother Earth blocked the explosion's force, enraged, the blast went upwards, ripping off the face of the building. Outer floors disappeared upwards in a black cloud mixed with glass, concrete, office furniture, bodies of people and flame. A textured black and orange plume rose slowly into the clear, pure morning sky. The explosion raged on, taking the three front pillars holding up the magnificent, black building and removing them. Slowly, the black office tower started to sag to its knees.

Destruction was complete, the office tower designed for withstanding earthquakes, could not withstand the tearing impact, the magnificent, black office tower crumpled completely as a planned demolition.

The explosion took a car parked on the street and decapitated it, throwing it at another vehicle passing by. Terrible force took the carcasses of both torn and crushed vehicles, embedding them in the building across the street. Corrupted by its total power, the energy rose to the sky, following the plume of black smoke and debris. The sky did not resist, it absorbed the energy, taking it out of the debris into itself, the black mass abandoned, hung there until gravity beckoned. Slowly it started to fall back to earth.

Greg Strome stood looking at the office towers standing like pillars against the fresh, morning sky, this day was a fresh start for him. After 10 years of copyrighting for an advertising firm, he left with bitter resentment they did not like the way he handled a large corporate account. A bitter dispute grew until the CEO got involved, offering threats to Greg's future. The fight became so ugly.

Greg left without any prospects and sat home for a week, struggling with depression. Monday morning, the phone rang. It was the Advertising and Marketing Director for the large corporation; he had apparently liked Greg's work. The director offered him a retainer; a decent budget and the rest became history. This morning the view from his new office was breathtaking, so was his future. He stood looking at the pillars and the city, the sun streaming in his window flooding him with new energy. Excitement building up inside of him joined hands with the fresh cup of coffee he was drinking. Greg felt more alive than he had ever been in his life. A bright future lay before him.

A rumble like thunder, he could not understand the sound, and then he could feel the tremor in the floor. The second before the fury of the explosion took him into itself, he actually saw the glass window disappear, the floor beneath his feet started to come apart. In his last moments, there was no pain, only total surprise, and wonder. Greg Strome disappeared forever into the fury of the explosion.

She sat looking at her computer screen; the long list of e-mails overwhelming, depression put a heavy weight in her arms and her soul. After a long string of arguments and increasing tension, her husband had thrown some clothing into a suitcase and left in anger. He had lost his job sometime ago and had not been able to replace it. It had not harmed them financially, but the emotional damage to her husband had been substantial. His self-esteem slowly drained away and depression flowed in to replace it. She watched him slowly wither away; the man she knew and dearly loved disappeared. Lisa Mitchell wanted her husband back desperately; her life was a shambles. She could not bear the empty, dark house every night, the pressure of her loss slowly building into desperation.

Lisa looked away from the computer screen, letting her eyes travel over the city and the new morning. Suddenly a surge of emotion rose in her, she had to get her husband back, she loved him, needed him. At this time, she did not know how, but knew she must do it. Emotion and motivation filled her as a fresh wind fills a sail. She would complete her day and call her husband, her, love.

Lisa had an office that was set back deeper into the building, away from the outer wall. The fury of the explosion flashing up the face of the office tower did not pull her into its vortex; instead, the side pressure entered her office and threw her body across the room. The shattered glass and razor sharp pieces of metal window frames followed the side pressure, they cut her to pieces, and she lay slumped against the wall cut, bleeding and broken. The sequence lasting only seconds, left Lisa shocked, and confused. When the body goes into shock, pain is in the distance. Lisa lay there, praying to wake up, it was a very bad dream; she did not want it anymore.

Slowly she started drifting away into darkness, happy that she was still asleep and the dream was going away. She died slowly, waiting for the dream to fade, morning to come.

Pete Taylor stood looking out of the window of his office. The black office tower across from his never failed to motivate him. In his mind, it resembled a mirage; it sparkled, mirroring the morning sun. Sipping his first coffee of the day, he would look out at the sky, the distant ocean, and the gleaming black tower. All the beauty and the moment of silence would allow him to put the pieces of his day together.

Slowly sipping his coffee, Pete looked away from the black, office tower; he heard the sharp crack of noise and a rumble resembling thunder. He could not understand it. Instinctively, he looked around for evidence of an impending storm. There were no clouds in the sky. His eyes darted back to the black tower; he could not comprehend the vision. It was unbelievable, a dream, a mistake. Red fire and black smoke were rising into the pristine, blue, morning sky. The plume textured, whorled with black, and red resembled a black flower opening it petals.

The entire face of the beautiful, black tower had become a black and red tinted cloud; it was slowly rising into the clear, morning sky.

Gripping his coffee cup, Conrad Taylor stood and watched a new morning suddenly transformed into an unbelievable scene from hell.

He watched the dying building falling to its knees, gently leaning and starting to slowly collapse. The structural steel started bending, unyielding concrete exploding into gray dust, exposing offices with people inside. They disappeared into the clouds of dust and debris. Slowly the black diamond of Seattle fell into the street.

Concrete, glass, and steel was raining from the pristine, blue sky. A few blocks away a woman on her way back to her office in the black tower stopped and started screaming, the sound was like some tortured creature. It went on and on until a man next to her walked over, gently turned her to face him and put his arms around her. She buried her face into his chest, muffling her screams. They stood there, the horrendous destruction framed in the distance.

As it fell, the tower glanced off another building, tearing away the facing, leaving an office exposed, a man inside unharmed, stood looking out in terror.

The surrounding area was in chaos. The noise of the explosion was gone, debris stopped raining from the sky, the gutted building was settling with occasional scraping and groaning of tortured metal. Silence came slowly, broken by occasional shouts from men and sporadic sobbing of women.

Then sharp wailing from sirens started; fire engines, police, and emergency personnel were arriving.

Hamid al-Issa stood looking down the canyon of towering buildings. He felt comfortable being a safe distance from the destruction. He heard the sharp crack of the blast and saw the rose-colored black plume rise slowly into the sky. Clenching his fists, his body stiffened. They would feel the hurt for a change.

CHAPTER – 8

A shrill, distant sound, like an endless throbbing pain tried to penetrate into the coma of sleep. Finally, Neil Chambers opened his eyes. He lay in bed trying to understand the darkness, the ringing continued, harsh, and meaningless.

Reality came in a sudden painful surge, depression closed around him like a clenched fist; Neil started to struggle, turning onto his side, away from the ringing telephone. Painful images in his mind, suddenly blossoming and telling him Ellen was gone, and he was alone in their dark bedroom.

Abruptly, the telephone stopped its ringing; the silence became heavy and solid, a part of the darkness of the room, Neil lay fighting to open the fist of depression.

He looked around the darkness; he saw the light. It was at the bottom of the curtains, making a bright line along the floor, he could not look away from the light.

Slowly, he eased himself upright and sat on the edge of the bed. The black hole of depression pulled at him. He sat struggling to go further into the rest of his life. Finally, the bright light along the bottom of curtains won the struggle. Neil felt a new force from somewhere inside him, he stood up and started walking toward the bright line of light.

Heavy curtains blocked out any light from the window, leaving the bedroom dark and indistinct, Neil and Ellen had liked it that way. Both had trouble sleeping, so the heavy curtains had been a mutual choice. Slowly walking barefoot across the soft, thick carpet, a memory suddenly appeared like a mirage. He could almost feel Ellen lying beside him; they were talking. He remembered the darkness was similar to being blind, increasing sensory feeling, their kissing, and caressing a sensual ecstasy. Then the memory started to grow sharp edges, cutting into him, causing pain. Neil reached the curtains and stood looking down at the bright line of light along the floor, struggling to find the strength to win the battle. Inhaling deeply he reached up and opened the heavy curtains, bright, blinding sunlight hit with an impact.

It was beautiful day with brilliant, blue-sky, pink blossoms on the trees lining the street and bright, healing sunlight.

Neil stood looking out at his neighborhood, the houses, well-kept lawns, and the sun reflecting from a neighbor's window, today it was a total mix of pleasure and pain. Beautiful mornings never failed to inspire Neil but this morning was an exception, it had the harsh, bitter taste of painful memories. He stood lonely and desolate depression tugging at him, trying to seep into his mind, weaken his resolve. It kept urging him to close the curtains, shut out the day, and hide in bed.

The telephone started ringing again, shattering the moment like glass, Neil stood for a microsecond, then turning he walked back into the room toward the telephone.

Picking up the receiver, he interrupted the telephone's shrill sound; a metallic voice called to him, "Neil are you there?" The insistent voice was getting louder. Depression abruptly opened its fist and Neil had his mind and body back, he recognized the voice, it was the director at FBI headquarters in downtown Seattle. Neil spoke, the words triggered more reality, and he took his first step forward into the rest of his life. "I am here," he said.

"We have a nightmare in downtown Seattle. There has been a massive explosion, an office tower is down!"

"I had second thoughts about calling you during your leave of absence, but I need you. There is a mountain of rubble downtown, the police think an enormous quantity of explosive had been used; they feel it could be an act of terrorism. I know this is your personal space and you need the time, but there is no one to replace you, please accept my apologies." The voice had become soft, gentle, and understanding, lifting his coma of sleep like fog before the morning sun. He could feel a tingle flowing through his body, lifting his coma of sleep and depression, his pulse rose rapidly, Neil Chambers was coming back.

"I'll be there as soon as I can." Neil could feel familiar strength flowing through him, it would carry him out of the dark abyss he had been living in since Ellen had died, and familiar routine of his job would feed and heal his mind. "Give me some details and the location, Oh, and get priority clearance with the Seattle police. Tell them not to trample too much, there may be some things left behind that could help us." Neil's strength of focus and training started like a powerful engine. He jotted down the details the director gave him then he hung up the phone and headed for the shower. The hot water also fed his energy, and it gave him fuel to face the day and take steps into his new life.

Stepping through the doorway of his house into the bright sunlight, fragrances of the new, spring day began penetrating into him. Inhaling deeply, Neil looked around his familiar street. A neighbor waved, prompting Neil to wave back. The simple act sent positive energy flooding through him. It was a beautiful day, losing Ellen was a painful wound, but now the pain not as sharp, a subtle distance gained. He loved her and the feeling would always follow him through life, a glowing spark that would burn and hurt forever.

Today, other forces were filling him, like wind in a sail, moving him forward into the rest of his life.

Traffic stood backed up on the causeway from Bellevue to Seattle. A mixture of commuters trying to reach their work and people made curious by the news on radio and television, curious to see the carnage. Turning on the emergency vehicle lights, Neil slid into the HOV lane, weaving in and out between vehicles, using his siren to prompt some vehicles to move aside. Slowly he struggled through to the downtown core of Seattle. Nearing the location the Director had given him, he could hear the coarse honks of fire engines and the wail of police cars. When he turned the corner of the street, a scene from hell blossomed in his windshield.

Two blocks away, there was a smoking mountain of rubble, the carnage piled up against other buildings; it had flowed like a river down other streets.

Stopping at the yellow tape police had placed around the nightmarish scene, Neil sat, frozen by the scene of horror before him. A tall, office, tower had been reduced to a huge pile of grey, rubble twisted steel girders stuck out like ribs from the still smoking mass. At the base of this mountain of destruction, there were vehicles lying on their roofs, covered with pulverized concrete, great chunks of concrete were embedded in the windshields of other flattened, dust-covered vehicles. A semi trailer lay on its side; powdered dust and an occasional boulder of concrete covered its huge body and multitude of wheels. A taxi stood on its tail, leaning against another damaged building; it looked as if a giant hand had taken the vehicle and placed it there. Closer to Neil, the pavement looked as if the skies had rained glass, it lay sparkling like diamonds in the morning sunlight.

It was absolutely more than the mind could imagine. In the midst of tall corporate towers, in downtown Seattle, crushed and broken remains of a dead building covered an entire city block. Firefighters, police and volunteers were scrambling all over the massive mound of destruction; he did not see the police officer walk up to his vehicle.

"Sir, I need to see your identification, this is a restricted area." The officer's voice tense, full of stress. Neil pulled his eyes away from the horror on the street and looked up at the police officer. His eyes were wide, reflecting the emotion that was running wild inside him. Windows into his soul, they showed the horror the man had seen.

A police officer serves on the front lines, defending the public, in situations where he has to "shoot to kill" someone and sometimes rescue a child or injured person, they become a paradox of positive and negative emotions. When he or she goes home at the end of shift there are times when their life will never be the same, they killed someone. Today, in the officer's eyes, Neil saw the ultimate horror. After all this man had seen and done in the line of duty, today he was shocked and stressed beyond comprehension. The officer stood looking down at Neil, their eyes locked, Neil saw stress push the man's right shoulder upward, his body language saying he could reach for his gun. Neil made a supreme effort to make his voice passive. "Officer, I would wonder if you can help me." There was a pause and the shoulder relaxed, the police officer stood looking at Neil.

"I am with the FBI Special Terrorism Unit; I have special clearance to the area. Can you check with your supervisor? Neil reached into his jacket pocket for his picture ID wallet, passing it through the window to the officer. He saw the man study the badge and picture, look at Neil's face. Passing the wallet back through the open window, he said, "Go on through Mr. Chambers and be careful, there is a lot of loose concrete, material still falling and there is broken glass everywhere." Neil got out his vehicle, thanked the officer then started walking toward the mountain of destruction.

Walking slowly, he looked around, observing overturned vehicles, gutted, and turned into carcasses. Opposite the site of destruction, an office tower was scarred and torn. The glass of its windows missing, it lay sparkling in the street. Concrete from the fallen black tower lay in trails leading away from the mountain of its carcass. There were ambulances, fire trucks and police cars everywhere. Medics were working on people who hit by debris from the blast or were severely in shock. No one in the building had survived.

Walking slowly, he saw firefighters on top of the mountain, trying to remove debris from an arm sticking out of the rubble. Looking down, he saw a sheet covering what seemed remains of a human body. As he walked closer, he the blood soaked, sheet outlining the details of the body under it. He could see a wisp of black hair, the sheet gave definition to one leg, the other was missing.

In his career, Neil Chambers had seen destruction and death but never as concentrated and graphic as this scene. He turned his eyes away from the body on the pavement and walked on.

As Neil slowly walked on, his eyes roved over the unbelievable destruction that lay before him, this would forever mark him. Never in his life had he witnessed such devastation, a whole city block lay in ruins. Where there had once stood a magnificent office tower, there now lay broken, grey concrete, steel girders were sticking through the concrete like brown ribs of a body. The dust still hung in the air like fog and white smoke still rising in a pillar into the pure, blue, morning sky.

He walked up to a man who stood looking at the men scrambling over the ruins, trying to find anyone living. Neil recognized him immediately; it was Paul Moden, chief of detectives for the city police, recognition was mutual.

"Hi Neil, heard you were down and out for a while. Please accept my sincere sympathies about your wife Ellen." Paul's voice was thick with stress. Neil thanked him, and then stood in silence waiting for the man to respond with more information. The silence between the two men continued, like the ticking of a clock, seemingly endless. Finally, Paul Moden spoke, "We don't have anything of consequence yet Neil. The Chief advised us to keep you in the loop. It looks like an Oklahoma City thing, but we do not know yet. I have never been involved in anything of this size; it is difficult to know where to start."

A man came running toward them, Neil recognized him as the city's crime forensics supervisor. The man was shouting something to Paul. Finally, they both could hear and understand his words, "Paul, I think we found something." Breathing heavily from the exertion of running, the supervisor stopped in front of the two men, unfolding a sheet of white paper, on the paper were black granules.

The man's breath came in gasps from the exertion; he held the white sheet of paper protectively. Paul and Neil looked at the black granules, waiting for the man's breathing to normalize. Finally the forensics supervisor spoke. "We found the carcass of a white, full size delivery truck, almost destroyed. Parts of truck's frame and box were still intact. Peculiar we could not find anything that could resemble a load the truck was carrying. A small corner of the truck box and frame were some distance from the building, in the small corner, we found pay dirt. These small granules look like unexploded fertilizer. Until we test them at the lab, I will try to guess that we have another Oklahoma City thing." His breathing was becoming normal.

Neil looked down at the ground and stood in silence. He could feel the tension riding up into his shoulders and the unspeakable word trying to seep into his mind. Terrorism, the unmentionable had come to his city. He looked up at the mountain of rubble again, wondering, who could conceive to do such a thing in a civilized society. The destruction was horrific and when the results came in, the loss of life would be enormous.

CHAPTER − 9

Monday morning Carla Black stayed in bed longer than usual, her thoughts chattering to her and impressions dancing like a movie on her closed eyelids. To escape, Carla slipped into her housecoat and made coffee. While it brewed, she stood and looked out of the window. The weekend had been a total, social failure. Saturday someone from her past telephoned, insincerity flowed out of the telephone as he tried to convince her that his needs were in her best interests. Carla politely suggested maybe another time, he understood, thinking she was having that feminine thing.

Standing at a window looking at the horizon, sadness seemed to press on her like a heavy weight. She was lonely; there seemed no escape. The coffee aroma became magnetic, pulling her away from the window. Building herself a cup of coffee, she stood sipping, deep in thought. Suddenly she looked up, as if finally regaining control over her brooding. She could feel the coffee giving her life, energy slowly seeping into her mind and body. Enjoying the coffee, she began focusing on her workday ahead; it shut out the pain of another lost weekend.

A long line of commuters greeted Carla; they were moving very slowly along the causeway from Bellevue, she sensed there seemed to be something wrong. Anxiety and stress started building so she turned on the car radio for some soothing music. A very emotional disc jockey, his voice rising higher and higher in pitch revealed some horrific destruction in downtown Seattle. Apparently, there had been an explosion; it destroyed a tall office tower. Not having seen the TV news about the office tower, the agitated voice on the radio describing the destruction seemed distant and remote. Disliking constant, bad news, Carla did not watch television on the weekends. Instead, she escaped into TV movies, drifting with happy themes of love, couples holding hands and walking into the sunsets

Looking out at the endless line or vehicles inching slowly toward Seattle, Carla could feel irritation rising like heat within her, triggered by an urgency to be at her office at the correct time. Tension dug its claws into her shoulders; she constantly felt her hands clenching the steering wheel, anxiety starting to radiate down her back, she could not seem to get comfortable in the seat of her car. Slowly the line of cars inched across the lake into the downtown area. Finally, to release some of the pressure, she reached for her cell and called her office. Reception answered, the voice seemed strained and unnatural. Carla explained her situation and reception informed her there were many calls coming in related to her situation, she would add Carla's call to the list. Carla ended the call and laid her cell phone on the passenger seat beside her. She could feel her body relaxing slightly, the pressure in her spine lifting. Sitting deeper in the seat, Carla drifted slowly toward the heart of the city.

Saleem awoke early, filled with excitement; he could feel closure from the bombing of the office tower. The act would certainly create chaos in the heart of America. He stood in the shower, hot spray tingling on his skin, excitement flowing through his body. Suddenly impatient, he turned off the shower and stepped out of the glass and gold enclosure, he had many things to do. Reaching for a thick, white towel he dried himself rapidly, his mind racing.

His mother had taught him integrity; he must pay Hamid al-Issa. The man had a family and needed money for survival, and he could be of further assistance. Saleem was inside America, the jihad was becoming successful, and there were many things to do, he felt an urgency to move forward.

Carla finally arrived at the bank building; tension had invaded her body to such a high degree that when she moved to get out of her car, stiffness was painfully evident in her shoulders, back and legs. She entered the building and saw her co-workers standing in groups, talking excitedly; offering a strained good morning to the groups, she hurried past them toward her office. A weekend of isolation left her withdrawn socially. Once inside her office, Carla closed the door and stood for a moment feeling the comfort of her quiet office slowly seep in. Sitting in her black, leather chair, she prompted her computer to come out of hibernation, it responded slowly, the monitor came alive with color and all her familiar shortcuts. Looking at the screen, she could feel the flow of routine coming back. Carla began to arrange her day, depression dissolving like early morning fog.

Saleem telephoned the bank trying to obtain an appointment with the woman that was his contact. A female voice answered the voice cold and distant. He asked if he could speak with Carla Black. The female voice was abrupt, advising him that Carla was unavailable. Saleem hung up the telephone, tightness spreading through his chest and shoulders; he sat looking at the thick, rich carpet in his hotel suite. The need to move in his planned direction was irresistible. Saleem sat deep in thought; suddenly he looked up, his eyes wide. The idea was plain and simple, he would appear at the bank, they would not refuse him, wealth always the lever of choice.

By midmorning, Carla was well into her planned day. Coffee she had been sipping was gone so she to the coffee machine for a refill. Suddenly she could hear a commotion in the reception area, she looked up and saw a man walking rapidly toward her office, the receptionist keeping pace, talking to him. She was trying to stop him from penetrating the offices deep in the building. Carla watched the pair coming closer; their direction seemed to be her office. Looking more closely at the man, she remembered. He had been in her office discussing the transfer of funds from the Middle East. A very good-looking man, well dressed, his expensive, masculine cologne had tickled at her. She remembered his evasive eye contact with her, excitement rising, Carla Black stood looking at the man walking rapidly toward her.

They stopped in front of Carla. Both of them wide eyed, looking at her. The receptionist spoke first. "Carla, I am sorry. This man insisted on seeing you now. I informed him that your day was solidly booked, but he just started walking toward your office." Carla stood and looked at the pair, the receptionist was highly agitated, her facial skin blossoming pink from the stress of the moment. She looked at the man and suddenly she remembered his name, Saleem dal Figar. He stood looking at Carla expectantly; he did not look away. His eyes were dark and deep a gateway to a universe hidden there. Carla felt emotion rising inside of her, and then her resolve and focus came to the rescue. She looked back at the receptionist. "Helen, I will handle this." The receptionist stood there, her eyes full of questions. Carla spoke again, "Thank you Helen that will be all." The receptionist gave Carla one last worried looked then turned and retreated rapidly down the hallway.

Saleem's voice interrupted the tense moment. "I must apologize, but my needs are most important. I have a business transaction that could be very profitable for your bank." He stood there looking handsome and very masculine, and then he spoke again, "to help you decide, I could also make it very profitable for you personally." Saleem stood looking at Carla, waiting for the financial lever to move the situation forward.

Carla did not hesitate; her personal integrity came to the rescue. She thought about her appointments for the day. Some reached their roots into large corporate clients; they would take the change personally and become offended.

Something forgotten and buried inside of her tugged at her resolve again, she was immensely attracted to this man standing in front of her. A battle started but her integrity was a powerful barrier. "I am sorry, but my appointments for the day cannot be changed. Many of these people have extremely busy schedules and the appointments have been made sometime ago, it would be very unfair and disruptive to my clients." Carla looked up at Saleem's face, her voice controlled; their eyes made contact and held. The man did not waver this time and that too pleased Carla. He seemed sensitive and strong to life's moments.

Saleem felt the barrier. The woman was right of course. Her clients were possibly influential and change would be destructive. Instantly he knew that his tactics should change. Saleem stood looking at Carla, she was extremely attractive, and suddenly he felt a flow of an idea. He would try the "American

Way" and offer her business and pleasure. He would ask her to dinner and they could still fill his business needs. Before he spoke, he took his eyes away from their hold with the woman. Looking down at the floor, Saleem made his offer. "I am extremely sorry for intruding into your business day. It is very insensitive. A simple money transfer is all that is required, but an apology to you is most important right now. Would an invitation to dinner be an appropriate apology? It must be a place of your choice of course. Would you be my guest?" He looked back up at Carla's face, waiting for her response.

Her decision took the time of a flight of Cupid's arrow, and it struck home. Carla looked at the man standing in front of her, her neglected personal needs and all the recent loneliness joined hands, making a circle she could not break. She hesitated as memories of a restaurant on the lake came rushing in. Earlier in her marriage, there had been good times, candlelight dinners, watching sunsets over the lake. Her heart was racing and Carla knew she had instantly become a prisoner of her loneliness and isolation, coupled with the handsome man standing across from her, the moment was fatal, she made her decision. Carla looked up at Saleem and said, "Yes I would like that." Reaching for her business card in its holder on her desk, she wrote down her home number and looking up into Saleem's eyes, she handed him the card. "Please call me when it is convenient for you."

CHAPTER – 10

Neil Chambers read the forensics report; the small, black grain found in the scattered parts of the white van was common fertilizer. This is an explosive of the times, inexpensive, easily obtained and very powerful when mixed with diesel fuel. The mixing is an unstable process, but the finished product is as powerful as any explosive used in modern warfare.

Looking into the distance, his thoughts searched for a trail, was this duplication of the Oklahoma City bombing by an angry individual or an act of terrorism? At this point, the only clues were the gutted and ravaged parts of the white van and the small grains of fertilizer found in them. Where was the clue? Security guards in the building did not exist anymore. What about the security company in charge of the office tower, would they have records, maybe paper trails? Maybe after an exhaustive search, he would find an angry employee who needed the bitter aftertaste of retribution. An act of terrorism was another matter; it is a well-planned exercise, leaving very little clues. Neil knew he could not ignore any small bit of information.

Neil looked out of his office window; the day was leaving, fading away, deserted by the sunlight. He took a deep breath, it seemed as if his chest could not expand far enough, he had an enormous task ahead of him. Finding the elusive piece of the puzzle that would reveal why someone would kill so many people, destroy a huge building in downtown Seattle, leaving chaos in the city's pulsing heart. Coupled with this immediate, seemingly impossible exercise, it was the end of the day and he had to go home to an empty house, Ellen would not be there. Neil sat and looked out of the window watching the sky change color, islands of purple tinted clouds stretching to the horizon. Buildings were changing texture, shadows deepening as the sunlight took its departure. Depression pulled at him, inviting him to enter its sadness. He fought back, the rest of his life loomed ahead of him like a deserted highway, lonely, and desolate. Taking another deep, almost painful breath, Neil closed the file, turned off his computer, and prepared himself emotionally for an evening of isolation and sadness.

Carla unlocked the door to her apartment, everything seemed changed, she was looking through different eyes, colors were brighter, her apartment was cozier, and the evening pictured through her window was soft and gentle. Energy flowed through her like a strong river. Leaning back on the door to close it, she stood for a moment looking around, feeling a comfort surrounding her; it felt good to be home. Standing with her back to the door, she drifted off into her personal distance. Saleem had excited her, colored her life with a new meaning. He was handsome and elusive, an evening and dinner with him tingled through her like electricity. Carla stood captured by this mirage of the restaurant, the table, the soft glow of candles; she seemed to strain forward, missing parts of her life that had been beautiful. Carla Black stood for a long time looking at the image, enjoying the intoxicating flavors of her emotions. Abruptly giving her head a shake, Carla wondered what was happening to her, the man was a client and she did not even know anything about him. Taking her first step forward into the room, Carla was back into her personal world, and she had to prepare for another lonely evening. She went about preparing dinner, completing the chores at the end of her day, she could not lose the electric tingle that followed her around the apartment.

Saleem showered and slid into bed, the sheets felt cool, and he felt very comfortable. Lights from other high-rise apartments and hotels nearby cast a soft glow into his room, deep shadows sculpturing his room, he luxuriated, his thoughts roaming. Satisfaction rose like a swell inside of him, the soft spot in America had been easy to find, the plan for the office tower had been so easy to execute. Everything they had needed accessible, his father taught him

well, money was the tool of choice. You could get anything in this country
with money and the Americans were soft and unsuspecting. Hamid al Issa
had been an enormous help, he lived in America and knew about the culture
and its weaknesses. Excitement giving him wings, Saleem turned his head
and looked out of the glass doors of his suite. Plans were swirling in his head
like birds. He was indeed a soldier for Allah, a sharp sword in his hands.

Stretched out in the comfortable bed, Saleem turned his mind to the rest of
his journey in America. He stretched his legs feeling the cool sheets, the flow
of comforting energy. His thoughts sorting the necessary arrangements, an
image of Carla Black suddenly appeared. Saleem stiffened and lay very still
looking at the image, her hair was soft, it clung to her neck, and cheeks, her
eyes were large and full of expression. When she spoke, Saleem remembered
how her lips moved, sensuous and moist. A strange, troubling feeling started
to flow through him. Lying very still, not to disturb the image, he absorbed
all of her. Carla had a slightly revealing style to her blouse, revealing the
cleavage to her breasts, the way her chest rose and fell, stirring something
very different in him. Suddenly the beautiful woman in the elevator entered
the emotional show, Saleem could feel her body, her buttocks pressed against
him, and the fragrance of a woman filled his nostrils. He could hear the
female voices on telephones, soft, alluring. Heaviness started filling his loins,
flowing through his body. Suddenly Saleem could feel Allah's eyes upon
him, he turned over on his side, away from dancing images, they would not
leave until he started a chant repeatedly, and finally Saleem fell into a trouble
sleep.

Hamid al-Issa also lay in bed, lights from the bedroom window cast long,
distorted shadows on the ceiling. His anger felt so full of closure that his body
seemed to float. The office tower had been a satisfaction he could never have
imagined, he showed the Americans there is a price for punishing him when
he had spoken out about the injustices in their country. In all of his life, he
had not felt such gratification. TV news revealed that local authorities had no
real clues on the bombing of the office tower. It left him with a warm comfort.
Saleem had telephoned and money was on its way. Suddenly, his wife's voice
interrupted flight of fantasy and elation. "Hamid, the place where you worked
is gone. You have quit your job and have not been looking for another, how

will we live? We have almost no money left from our savings. Many nights I cannot sleep because I am frightened." Hamid did not move and he did not answer for what seemed a long time. Then, his mind full of conviction, he said, "It is not your business, there is money coming, it will be here shortly. Do not go where a woman cannot possibly understand." He abruptly felt a wall between them and turned on his side facing the light from the window, irritation flowed through him, his happiness, his plans interrupted with her petty thoughts.

Roya lay quietly for a long time; finally, she could hear her husband fall asleep, his breathing change and become deeper. Alone in the dark bedroom, her fear pulled at her, bitterness rose from the wall he had created with his hard words. She remembered how he had been so intense when the evening news was on TV. She had tried to speak to him, he had not turned from the television, just raised his hand to silence her. In silence she had watched him, an unknown fear rising. The emotional burden became a staggering weight, the sleepless nights robbing her energy until she felt her life was slipping away. What had her husband done? An ambulance was wailing in the distance, the sound like the keening of a woman. Roya related to the sound, like the wailing of a woman from her homeland, a pitiful sound of anguish when a child or a loved one is lost, Roya bonded to the sound. She was losing something but she did not know what. The morning light was seeping in through the bedroom window when, exhausted from fear and worry she finally drifted into a troubled sleep.

CHAPTER - 11

Carla Black woke with a start; she could sense something different. Her week had been extremely busy; the destruction of the office tower had everyone in downtown Seattle struggling to stay ahead of chaos.

As she lay there, sleep slowly dissolved like early morning fog, memories of the past week reeling through her mind like a movie. Clients drifted in and out, triggering no special meaning, Carla turned on her side to relieve built up pressure. Morning light was coming through the curtains of her bedroom window. Habitual sadness kept softly tugging at her, suddenly an image of a man burst through, Carla sat upright in bed.

Today was Saturday and she had a dinner date with the handsome man.

Energy flashed through her like lightening, Carla threw back the covers and jumped out of her bed. The strong flow of energy carried her to the window. The morning sun flooded in when she threw back the curtains, she could feel its subtle warmth on her face. She stood there, eyes closed, letting the golden glow enter her body. The power rising within her forced her eyes open. They rose to the fluffy white clouds in the sky. Today, the clouds did not look like lonely, desolate islands stretching into the distant blue horizon. They were sensuous, tinted with pinks, blues, and grays, radiating karma of good things to come.

It was a beautiful morning, Carla felt alive and inspired.

Tonight was dinner at her favorite restaurant with a handsome, mysterious, and very elusive man. She had tried to make eye contact. He looked away; a thrill passed through her again.

The day was a blur, full of activity and suddenly she was standing in front of her full-length mirror.

The woman that stood looking back at her had auburn hair, styled short accenting her green eyes. Her facial features were slim blending with full, red lips. She was wearing an elegant black dress that revealed a sensuous, feminine figure; it drew your eyes down to elegant, high-heeled shoes

It had been such a long time since she had dressed for pleasure, Carla almost could not recognize the beautiful woman looking back at her.

She had taken extreme care to fashion the woman standing there, Carla like what she saw.

Saleem sat across the table from Carla, the sunset made her hair a richer, darker red, the candlelight made her eyes mysterious. This was a beautiful, seductive woman dressed in a forbidden way. It was more than his will could control, even his eyes would not obey him.

A man's voice suddenly interrupted the silence between them, "Would you like some wine with dinner?" The waiter stood waiting for their answer.

Trapped in silence, drinking in his country is a forbidden act. Carla came to his aid, "Yes I would like some red wine." She furtively glanced at Saleem; he was looking down at his plate. On special occasions he took a drink at business occasions, it had been exciting and arousing. He looked up at the waiter, "Do you have a red merlot?"

The waiter was crisp and efficient, "Yes I have a local that is very good, I will be back with your drinks shortly." He turned smoothly, leaving Saleem and

Carla at their table, exposed to the sunset. The sunset gently created a mood that was to be destiny.

Saleem's eyes had developed a will of their own, leaving him very uncomfortable. They furtively kept glancing at the beautiful woman sitting across from him. Struggling for control by glancing at the lake colored with the sunset. Furtively, he glanced at Carla; the soft candlelight shadowed her face, darkening her hair, making it richer. The departing sun glowed on the attractive woman, softening her skin tones, making her more sensuous and alluring.

Slim straps held up Carla's dress, leaving her neck and shoulders bare. The low-cut dress took advantage of the sunset, enhancing the fullness of her cleavage. All this was more than Saleem had seen, conditioning by his mother and their culture dictated that a man should not look at a woman this way. For a moment the childhood barriers won, Saleem looked back out of the window. The sun had dropped lower, the colors of the lake and trees had deepened.

Simulating all people on their first meeting, Carla and Saleem exchanged a few casual words not related to anything. Silence would take over again making both feel more comfortable cloaked in it.

Carla glanced at Saleem also colored by the sunset and flickering candlelight, his features clean and masculine. Since her marriage had failed, she had lost herself in work, enduring painful, lonely weekends. Now surrounded by the lovely evening, some of her feminine instincts seemed to come out of hiding.

Gently sipping her wine, she glanced around the restaurant; a woman at the next table delicately fingered the stem of her wine glass, her eyes lowered demurely. The man across from her, very magnetized by her presence was passionately trying to convince the attractive woman of something.

Carla's gaze drifted further, on the other side of the room another couple were enjoying something humorous, their faces radiating laughter and pleasure. Candles sparkled like evening stars everywhere. People were enjoying the food and each other in the romantic atmosphere. Carla felt an emotional surge within her; she had forgotten the flavors of companionship. She looked back at Saleem. He was looking out of the window; she sensed he could not or would not look at her.

Carla felt an almost forgotten, feminine thing she had not felt in a long time, jealousy.

Very attracted to the man at her table, Carla needed to feel his attraction for her, picking up her glass of wine; Carla broke the silence between them. "What do you do in your country when it is a special occasion and there is wine at your table?"

Confronted by the eyes of a very beautiful woman, he said, "What would you like to do?"

Raising her glass higher, Carla extended it toward Saleem. Watching her example, he raised his ruby colored glass of wine, both hesitated for seconds, and then Saleem leaned over and they touched wineglasses.

The crystal chimed like a silver bell, they each took a sip of wine, their eyes meeting this time.

Drinking was a paradox to Saleem and today the wine opened the door to a hidden part of him. He became more confident, sat deeper into his chair, and met Carla's eyes more often. Looking closer, he saw how makeup had enhanced them; her eyelashes were fuller, darker, enhancing her green eyes. Customs are very strong and they tried to come to his rescue, his inhibitions fought to regain control. Saleem sipped more often and the wine won the battle, making everything more beautiful.

The sunset took its colors, leaving behind the deep midnight blue sky, a signal for the tiny, distant stars to come forward. The silence between them lost its hold; they talked more about casual things.

Carla let her eyes wander around the restaurant, a distant need gently pushing at her. The waiter brought their dinners, aware of their mood, became a shadow, quietly serving them. Tiny candles that had filled the room gained strength, deepening shadows making everything mystical. Soft chatter of other guests, the clink of glasses and silverware turned the evening into a spiritual passage.

Standing at Carla's door, both of them were different, more relaxed. Then like a continuous passage of moods, a new hunger rose in both of them, its growing force making them restless. The evening breeze took Carla's fragrance and softly carried it to Saleem; he inhaled deeply as if to fill himself, a strange need growing. For the first time in his existence, he stood looking down into a woman's eyes, enjoying the flow into himself. Saleem did not understand, but he knew there was a change in him forever.

His words were gentle, soft, "Thank you for a wonderful evening." Carla looked up at the handsome man standing before her, "It was my pleasure," she reached out and took Saleem's hand. A force passed between them, their hands the bridge, both felt the sudden disturbance within their bodies.

Unable to take their first step into destiny, they stood holding hands, looking into each other's eyes. Suddenly on impulse, Carla stood on her tiptoes, leaned forward, and kissed Saleem on the cheek; his masculine fragrance flowed into her. The elusive woman living in Carla took over the moment; Carla pulled her hand away and moved toward her doorway. Saleem watched her insert the key, open the door; then the beautiful woman and the moment vanished like a dream. He stood looking at the closed door; slowly he walked back to his car.

During the moody drive back to the hotel, Saleem could still feel the spots on his chest where Carla's breasts had left two points of heat.

Deep in thought, night city lights and shadows flickered in his car. His plan for America was stronger than ever, he needed to be with the woman again.

Carla lay in her bed. It was suddenly different, too big for her. She stretched her legs through the cool sheets, reaching with her toes, searching the empty bed. Closing her eyes was a signal for the flashback waiting. She could smell the masculine cologne; feel Saleem's hand and the flow of need passing between their hand bridge. The memory of her breasts pressing against his hard chest rushed in. Carla could not lay still, a need pulled at her.

Laying there in the darkness of her bedroom, Carla decided she had to see Saleem again.

CHAPTER – 12

Neil Chambers got out of his car and walked up the driveway to his house, singling out the key for the front door. He stopped and stood looking at the key for a moment; abruptly he inserted it into the lock, opening the door. He stepped inside, the door closed behind him with a soft click. Silence filled the house, late afternoon sunlight streamed through the big window in the front room. Sunlight seemed to have a different meaning now, sadness started to close on him like a heavy cloak. He looked up the flight of stair leading to the bedrooms; there was no one there to greet him. Ellen had always been there, like a mirage of beauty, shining into his life.

The stairs were empty.

Neil stood alone in what once was "their" home, unable to move, depression filling him like a cold fog rushing inland. He looked once more into the living room, and then up the stairs, she was gone forever. With a sigh, he took the first step into an empty house.

Changing from his suit to his old favorites, jeans and a casual shirt, he began wandering through the house, searching and looking for something, an appetite for dinner. There was nothing, no one; the silence in the house was solid. He sat in the living room and looked at the setting sun making patterns of light on the furniture, a bright spot on the carpet; it gave him a lonely, desolate feeling.

Neil sat there, deserted by energy and motivation, no place to go, the rest of his life to do it.

Reaching for the TV remote, Neil turned on the television, evening news reeling out at him, and media were now struggling with a dying story about the bombing. No matter how much life they tried to breathe into the story, there was nothing new to add, it was fading. Investigation of the downtown bombing was struggling, forcing Neil to assign all the FBI staff to the case. Sorting through bits of evidence, they eventually would wind up in blind alleys. All they had at this time was that the explosive material was common fertilizer mixed with diesel fuel, easily purchased. Destruction of the truck had been complete; the VIN number on the dash had probably evaporated from the destructive force. Security for the building had nothing to contribute; the guard on duty killed, staff records yielded nothing, the investigation was at a standstill.

He turned to another channel; an old western rerun flickered at him. Rapidly losing interest, he directed his attention to the stereo and found his favorite music station. Soft music flowed out filling the room. Once he had loved the station and its selections, today it could not seem to reach him. He sat looking at the light fade slowly; the sun seemed to be leaving him also.

Sensors started turning on streetlights, their pale, yellow tinted light shone in through windows on the empty street. The yellow light found Neil still sitting in his chair. Deep in thought, he searched for that elusive piece of the puzzle that would put his life back together. He had not eaten, his preoccupation was a solid enclosure, and it even kept out hunger. Suddenly the telephone rang the sound loud and harsh in the semi-dark silence of the house. It rang several times, seeming to get louder and more insistent when Neil did not move. He sat looking out of the window at the gathering dark outside; reality was abrupt forcing him to pick up the receiver.

It was a call from someone at his office, Neil could not immediately recognize the excited voice, and its words seemed meaningless. Finally, the electronic voice stopped, there was silence for a second, and then voice probed. "Did you hear what I just told you? The voice was again becoming excited, we found the truck's bumper, there was a license plate attached, the recess in the bumper protected it. The plate was scorched and burned, but the letters are raised, we can get a registration through DMV."

Neil could hear the words; they seemed familiar. He had been deep in depression from the empty house. It was like seeing someone or something, but at that moment, the mind cannot relate to anything, connections in his mind seemed to be missing.

"Neil, you okay?" Sound from the telephone was highly agitated, partially from the excitement of the news the person wanted to relate and partially from being unable to get closure, the person intended was not receiving its message. Again, "Is anyone there?" Finally, possibly the sound had become insistent enough to trigger something in his conscious mind and Neil responded. "Yes, everything is okay; I was just having a nap before dinner."

"Did you hear what I just told you Neil? We found the truck's bumper, now we are able to do a search, find the owner to the truck and consequently, who was driving it. This is a major breakthrough for us." The voice belonged to one of his assistant investigators.

The sudden drift of focus from the pain of missing his wife brought Neil back; he could feel the sharp, heady surge of adrenaline. His mind began racing, tracking and sorting through the evidence they collected, there had been very little for them to move forward. He wondered who could have such an enormous grudge or hatred to destroy huge office building and kill so many people. When he thought about the amount of hatred, it would take, Neil could feel a black pit with no bottom, and he could not see an answer.

Abruptly, the voice interrupted his thoughts again. "Neil, are you still there?" It brought him back to the immediate. "Process the new information and please keep me in the loop all the time, day, or night. Get on it, find these people." The new information was surging through him like a wild river. He stood for a moment feeling the new excitement, mixed with direction, to find the person or persons responsible for the bombing, killing people.

Suddenly he did not feel alone in his grief. Others had suffered a tremendous misfortune; they lost their loved ones, their lives altered eternally. Neil had to help them get closure. He moved toward the kitchen, he knew that by helping all the people who had been hurt, it would help him heal. Directing his efforts to create meal, his thoughts flashed in the new storm in his mind. He would always love Ellen; she would be a light that would never go out. Neil Chambers moved forward into the rest of his life, vowing to remember the beautiful woman that had touched him forever.

In another part of the city, Hamid al Issa was elated; he was flying with excitement, pleasure, and closure as he watched the evening news, the local police and the FBI had no evidence, it was a dead end. Hamid had not felt such pleasure about anything since he had come to America. This culture troubled him, but today, he was on a high, convinced that being a soldier for Allah was the best decision he had ever made. They had a lesson they would never forget. Sitting back in his favorite, easy chair, stretching his legs out, Hamid could feel pleasure flowing through him. The familiar odors of his wife's cooking drifted in from the kitchen area, increasing his comfort. It was good to be alive.

CHAPTER - 13

The rear bumper of the white van lay on the table in the FBI forensics lab it was twisted and scorched. The explosion had sheared the bolts holding it onto the truck frame and literally blown it away. All truck manufacturers make a recess in the bumper for a license plate; it had protected the plate when the force from the explosion had reached around trying to destroy the plate. Inside this recess, still attached was the license plate, scorched black from the horrendous heat, its secret could not be destroyed, the raised lettering would tell who owned the truck.

FBI forensics staff stood gathered in a group around the table, their silence showing reverence to the gift bestowed upon them, hope surged through the group. They lived to find secrets that would punish individuals who administered pain onto society. Now the pressure released, they could all move on, completing their tasks, getting personal closure.

Neil Chambers, part of the group, also stood silently looking at the new direction the investigation had taken. He could feel his personal pain receding and was feeling better this morning.

The FBI director broke the silence, "Well people, you are looking at the beginning of the end for someone. Go to work and see where the numbers on the plate lead us."

The sudden words stirred the silent group like leaves by a gust of wind, they turned and scattered, each focused on their personal direction and duty.

Again, the director spoke, this time his voice was louder to catch the retreating members of the group. "Please coordinate everything with Neil. He is leading the investigation. In addition, the news media will be on us like vultures at a feeding frenzy. Keep a lid on the new lead, no leaks please, people. Let's go to work."

Feeling very elated, Hamid al-Issa telephoned Saleem at his hotel. He needed money for his family and some promise of a new and more secure future. Saleem assured him that all was well and money was just around the corner. Both felt very high, elevated from their recent endeavors. They chatted about creating more pleasure for Allah, something bigger that would attract the attention of America. Each had personal motivation humming through them; they agreed to meet again in a very short time.

Hamid al-Issa's wife watched from the other room, she could not totally understand the meaning of the conversation, her husband was very careful, choosing his words, aware of her presence. In her woman's way, she could sense something was dreadfully wrong. Her husband was out of work; the building where he was a security guard had been bombed and destroyed. She turned and looked out of the window at the blue sky and the distant horizon, something terrible was coming, she could almost feel its presence now. As a child, Roya remembered her homeland and the moods of the desert. Just before a sandstorm that lasted for days, killing animals and sometime people, the sky was the purest blue, a peace over the land, then without warning the storm hit.

She looked up at the blue sky; her gaze dropped to the distant horizon and suddenly she could feel the presence of something terrible waiting in the distance, waiting to sweep a terrible destruction on her small family.

News reeled out; there were robberies, a woman beaten by an intruder and a fatal accident on the freeway, it was consistently the same, lulling Hamid into a kind of lethargy. Pictures on the TV started drifting out of focus and the sound of the woman's voice slowly becoming a distant monotone; he lay back deeper into his favorite chair. All precautions taken, no clues left behind to reveal his identity, they would never find him. He had paid cash for the truck rental, a very wise move; explosive material used was untraceable. Hamid layback, his body relaxing, he drifted to that soft, comfortable drop into a nap before dinner, his mind traveled over the bombing. Slowly his mind traveled over the details, pictures in his mind. He was just about to enter his nap when a picture of the truck rental reeled out again. The people at the rental said they were comfortable with cash if he purchased insurance, they would however require a look at his driver's license. The clerk had taken Hamid's license, looked at it for a moment, and then handed it back. As he was putting the license away in his wallet, Hamid noticed something; the clerk had written a series of numbers down on the rental form.

Hamid al-Issa bolted upright from him comfortable position. Panic raced through his body, they would find him. His driver's license had all the necessary details, his picture, his home address, a trail directly to him. Hamid al-Issa had been a police officer in his homeland, training, internal politics and truths trained him well, made him very streetwise.

He knew he was in trouble; he must contact Saleem and discuss serious money that would allow him to leave America for a safe haven.

Amid the sudden hurricane of emotion, Hamid remembered his wife and child. How could he escape burdened with a woman? Where could he go? Certainly not back to his homeland, too much hardship waited.

Suddenly America seemed very good, opportunity everywhere; he could have risen financially here. Everyone on his job had talked about it being the land of opportunity. Looking back, he saw how comfortable it had been. His apartment was meager but a good deal better than the conditions he had lived in before coming to America. Hamid's thoughts traveled back to his job as a security guard; suddenly he realized that speaking out about America had been wrong. His wages in America were meager but in comparison to wages back home, they were wealth. Life here had not been so bad. Suddenly Hamid loved America and wanted to stay more than anything he had ever wanted in his life. Stress flowed through him like a river out of control.

Hamid's wife watching from the other room saw her husband suddenly leap from his favorite chair, moving rapidly he picked up the telephone and began dialing. She had watched him change; her husband was not the same man anymore. At mealtime, he had become serious, eating silently, without the same emotion. He had been excited about coming to America, then talking about his job, how he would change things if he could. He had insisted that he knew better. Suddenly one day he became different, quiet, often skipping his favorite TV programs to telephone people, speaking to them quietly, his words picked carefully so she could not understand. Even though not allowed to discuss a man's affairs because she was a woman, in her woman's way she knew something was wrong.

The tightness in her chest slowly spread upwards until her mouth felt dry; there was a tremble in her back and legs. She watched her husband speak to someone about a meeting. Some of his words were "soon" and "very important." Her husband hung up the telephone much harder than usual, then turned and sat back in his chair. Quietly she moved around doing women's work, but out of the corner of her eye, she saw her husband sitting staring at the floor, the television that he loved was unnoticed.

The karma of the storm she was expecting was stronger, the storm closer. There was something coming to harm the family.

CHAPTER - 14

Saleem and Hamid agreed to a meeting at the park where they had their first successful encounter, a park near the apartment where Hamid and his family lived.

Parking his car, Saleem waited, he tried to understand why Hamid had been so upset on the telephone. All had gone well with the bombing of the office tower; everything had gone according to plan. Saleem was convinced they had not missed anything.

He looked up and saw someone come out of the apartment building across the street, it was Hamid. He watched as the man walked toward him, his stride long and very rapid. In a very short period of time Hamid stood before Saleem, his eyes mirrored the storm raging within him, their eyes met and held, Hamid stood without speaking; abruptly he looked away into his personal distance. Without turning his head, he suddenly spoke.

"We are in serious trouble. They will discover us shortly." Hamid turned his head, his eyes troubled, his face distorted by the stress he carried.

His mind racing in a frantic search, Saleem went over the plans for the bombing, they did not miss any detail had been examined repeatedly. He did not understand the fear that Hamid was radiating. Saleem looked at Hamid, their eyes colliding and holding.

"You are wrong. There is nothing to fear. You are a soldier for Allah and you must be strong, have courage and patience until the next time we hit them."

Hamid broke their eye contact, looked away again. "There will not be a next time for us; we made a fatal error, a small thing. They are soft but eventually they will stumble onto the mistake, it will point its finger at us. Many years as a police officer, I have learned these things. The mistake was a small thing, but they will find it." He stopped speaking and did not turn his head back to look at Saleem. Fear and shame had taken over the man completely. Hamid stood in silence, looking away into the distance.

Saleem spoke with conviction, "to be soldier for Allah there is sacrifice, courage is necessary and dedication is a must. One must totally be without fear, cold like the steel of a sword. It is often necessary to sacrifice someone or many in order to help many. Are you afraid to serve Allah?" The question was hard; the answer could only be harder, a spear that would penetrate Hamid's manhood. He had not moved, still looking away into the distance. Saleem stopped talking; he stood looking at Hamid, waiting for the difficult answer.

This time the silence was longer, becoming uncomfortable. Hamid could feel his shame closing in on him like a heavy cloak. He should have known better, after all, he had been a police officer, a good one. A small mistake had cost him his future, the rest of his life. The Americans would hunt for a long time, his life ruined. Finally, his pride came to the rescue, whispering to him. Without turning his head to look at Saleem, he spoke. "It is easy for you to talk of courage, you are one of the blessed ones, and your family is rich. It is easy to fight fear when you have money and can buy safety and peace of mind. You can stand proud as a soldier for Allah; your money is your shield. For me, there is nothing to show but a life of hardship and a wife and child. I have no money to protect or hide me. You promised money, a job, and security. Today, I need you to keep your promises."

Hamid was stalling; he was having trouble revealing he made the unforgivable mistake. If he could just turn this around, use some kind of pressure to get money, it would secure his future. His head was full of thoughts, whispers, suggestions that could turn his disaster around.

Abruptly, Saleem started walking toward his car. Hamid heard the movement, steps on the gravel of the path leading to the street. His chance for survival was leaving, his thoughts became frantic, and the whispers in his head were desperate. He could feel his heart trying to hammer a path through his chest. He stood helplessly and watched Saleem reach the car and open the driver's door. Suddenly he knew he had to forget his pride, and get his money, "Wait," he shouted. Holding the door of his car open, Saleem stood looking at Hamid questioningly.

"Wait, come back and we will talk, I will tell you." Saleem stood for another second then he slammed the car door shut and began to walk back to Hamid.

Hamid watched Saleem return, he felt the loss; it was his self-esteem, his dignity. This time he did not turn his head away, there was too much at risk, he was desperate, frightened. Finally, Saleem stood in front of Hamid, their eyes locked. Hamid's thoughts chattered to him, out of control, he searched for the first words to release his hidden truth, the other man's eyes cold and accusing. Hamid had always been able to ease himself out of situations.

He had nowhere to hide from his truth. "I made the mistake and nothing can change it now. It is a small mistake but they will find it." He stood struggling with his remaining pride. "I need the money to leave this country, to be safe somewhere. They will look for a long time and they will find my mistake." The outburst about his shame released, he looked away and stood in silence his heart hammering in his chest, a sick feeling of shame spreading slowly through him.

"What is the mistake? There will be no money unless I know what problems we have to face." Hamid heard Saleem's fatal words and knew he must bring the truth out into daylight and reveal his shame.

"Everything went according to plan, nothing was missed. They will never find the people who mixed the fertilizer; the truck was shattered into small pieces.

There was one small mistake. I paid cash for the truck rental, but there is one detail. Hamid was struggling uncomfortably, he heard Saleem's feet shift on the gravel of the path, he knew it was time to reveal the truth.

"When I rented the truck, they wanted to see my driver's license. If I had refused, they would not have given me the truck. The clerk looked at it and he wrote a number down. I have been a policeman and I know they will find me."

Saleem stood for a moment, deep in thought, searching for the answer to the rest of his jihad. The discovery of Hamid would make a path that would lead directly to him. All the plans ended; his resolution of anger would not have satisfying closure. A secret thought suddenly whispered to Saleem, he turned and looked at Hamid, thinking and studying him, the thought whispering. To destroy the man would still leave a great deal of effort, then there was Hamid's wife, she could complicate matters. They would keep looking, complicating his mission. To pay him, would create a dead end for the authorities, it would leave no one to question. Saleem still looking at Hamid suddenly smiled, "I will pay you, reward you even though you failed, and made a mistake that could have destroyed the mission."

Hamid felt a sudden release surge through his body, as if he had known how close he had come to death.

Driving back to his hotel, Saleem traveled over his thoughts and plans. He had made a good decision. In between his father's rages, he had learned that sometimes it is good business to pay good money to bury a bad decision. He felt a satisfaction that the man would not be part of any other plans.

The time had come to contact his father regarding money. Saleem was living on credit cards, but large amounts of money needed now to pay associates, motivate them, to pay for goods and services.

He would contact his father and Carla, set up a flow of money in a holding account. Turning the corner of the street, the comfortable sight of his hotel stood before him.

Saleem was excited to get on with his plans, to contact his father, which in turn would give him a reason to see Carla again.

Disturbing thoughts started to nudge at his mind. Saleem had never touched a woman intimately before in his life. In his country, all women were covered, their hair, their lower face, the hijabs they wore did not reveal their body shapes. One did not look into their eyes it was disrespectful. These thoughts were trampling his plans for the rest of his mission. They were bad, disrespectful thoughts, but secretly he liked them. He enjoyed the visions of Carla sitting at the table, the candlelight revealing the shape of her bosom, her slender arms, delicate fingers that curled sensuously around the stem of a wine glass. As he drove, he could see her face, her furtive, beautiful green eyes. The setting sun had turned her auburn hair on fire; it glowed redder, more beautiful. Saleem could still feel the burning touch of her breasts as she had leaned over to kiss him on the cheek, still feel the spots on his chest now.

Saleem changed position in the leather seat of his BMW, an unfamiliar heaviness in his thighs.

CHAPTER – 15

Ellen was excited, pulling Neil's arm and chattering something about "beautiful babies." The San Diego Zoo was crowded, families on vacation with their children eating ice cream cones and looking excitedly at the caged animals. Finally, Ellen succeeded in tugging Neil to a cage that contained leopard. It was apparently a female; there were tiny, newborn kittens in the cage with her. The female lay quietly in the sun. Her body was completely relaxed, her eyes alert. The leopard's eyes never left the people gathered around her cage, the tip of her tail never stopped flicking back and forth.

Ellen loved new babies of all kinds. Anything newborn was beautiful to her. She stood in front of the cage, tightly holding Neil's hand, watching the baby leopards perform. They were fuzzy energy balls learning to fight, bite, and snarl. Neil had to admit they were extremely cute. He stood there feeling the tightness of Ellen's hand, its energy flowing up his arm to his heart. She still captivated him, turning his world into a soft, wonderful place. The same tightness of her hand seemed to make his heart ache; Neil Chambers was totally in love with his wife. It was a beautiful morning; the sun was pure gold, shining on the world, making trees, buildings and the pristine sky mystical.

Their dreamlike vacation would leave memories with him forever.

Neil stood holding his wife's hand feeling as if he was the luckiest man in the whole world then suddenly a telephone started ringing, he turned around, trying to find the origin of the sound. People's faces turned toward him, their eyes wide. The irritating sound of the telephone persisted. Neil turned to look at Ellen, she was gone, and he could not feel her hand anymore. Panic started to rise in his chest, he turned his head, and all the people were gone, the cage was empty, the leopard, her babies were gone. The telephone kept ringing and ringing, he wished it would stop so he could go and look for Ellen.

The telephone ringing was getting louder, it was on his left side. Neil decided the only way to stop the ringing was to answer the phone; he turned reaching for the sound. Like a bursting soap bubble, dream disappeared. Recognizing his bedroom, Neil looked around; he was alone in bed. Reaching over he picked up the telephone, instantly the ringing stopped.

He heard a loud, excited voice, "Neil, we found the link to the bombing." It was one of his associate investigators working with him on the case. "I apologize for calling so early, but I thought you would like to know. This is our first substantial break. The truck was a rental and the company did not report it. We called them and talked to the manager and he stated that this happens a great deal. They have the name of the individual who rented the truck, he paid cash, but they recorded data from the driver's license. We have them cornered and I know that you would like to deliver the surprise in person." There was silence on the line.

Neil absorbed the valuable information, savoring the emotional closure, and then abruptly he spoke to the caller. "You made my day; I will be at the office shortly." He could feel a sudden surge of energy enter his body, striking him like a small bolt of lightning, adrenaline flowed through him like a river, and he headed for the shower.

The truck rental company was near the airport, the manager a younger man. Police or an FBI agent had never confronted him. When Neil showed his identification, the manager's face suddenly flushed pink, he broke eye contact with Neil, and his customer service face disappeared. After Neil provided him with the information he needed, the manager looked through his rental contracts, he found Hamid's contract and placed it on the counter, hands slightly trembling. Neil rapidly looked over the contract. It contained a company name, which of course would be false, the information about the driver the key, the secret. Looking up the manager, Neil said, "You did an excellent job."

Looking at Neil, his customer service face started to reappear like the sun breaking through the clouds, his shoulders dropped slightly as his internal pressure released. Neil turned abruptly and headed for the door, the contract in his hand, "we will be in touch," he said over his shoulder.

The offices for the security company that had monitored the office tower were in another part of the city. They were responsible for many such projects in the city and the state. Well organized, their employee pool was enormous. Neil sat in the office of the General Manager, a placid, overweight man who sat looking at a computer printout of employees; suddenly he looked up at Neil. "Yes we had an employee by the name of Hamid al-Issa working for us. We hired him because he had excellent credentials; he was an ex-police officer in the Middle East. Recently, we passed him over for a promotion to supervisor. There are some notes here from the Personnel Department. He was quite outspoken about the United States. They state here that he was a good worker, but did not have leadership skills, his negative attitude was his downfall." The general manager leaned back in his black, leather chair, exposing his huge stomach. "He is no longer employed by us, he resigned recently," the man tilted his head, looking at Neil; his huge stomach had stopped moving from the effort of speech. "We have an address listed, I don't know if it is still valid."

Neil took out a small notebook he carried and wrote the information as the man spoke. "That is all there is," the general manager sat looking at Neil. "What is all this about?"

Neil put away his notebook and stood up, "Your help is appreciated, we are looking at some information that could be helpful," he said, turning to leave. The fat general manager stood up with great effort, his stomach pulling and distorting his white shirt.

Extending his hand to Neil, he said, "If I can be of any further assistance, please do not hesitate to call on me."

Sitting in his car, Neil took out the small notebook and looked at the address written on the page. He could feel excitement building; he had an address. Leaning back against the headrest, he turned his head and looked out at the flow of traffic on the street. The information fit the puzzle, an unhappy police officer from another culture, angered by losing a promotion to more power, traditional history that often triggered anger, and the pathway to revenge. He sat looking out of the window, not seeing the traffic, his eyes focused on a personal distance, he could feel a slight closure; his work was putting his life back together.

Saleem noted fatigue in his father's voice; so he did not go into pleasantries or the usual family member exchange, blocked by emotional barriers and a deep river of anger that flow through him. Its energy would be there for as long as they both lived.

The telephone conversation lasted for some time as they discussed business possibilities in America. Saleem offered a positive tone; it did not alter his father's energy or enthusiasm. His father did agree with the lawyer's suggestions, the prospect of registering a corporation in America, Saleem giving it direction. They discussed money and Saleem's father again agreed, open to any amount Saleem required. Without any negatives in the conversation, they agreed on one million US dollars as seed capital. Finally, Saleem asked about his mother. His father was silent for a moment, and then he said, "She is fine and sends her best wishes." Abruptly he excused himself, stating there was an urgent matter that needed his attention. He also added that Saleem should set up the necessary paperwork and contact him when it all was ready for a money transfer. The phone went dead and Saleem sat listening to the dial tone, tightness in his chest that had a painful edge to it. Finally, he hung up the telephone and sat looking out of the glass doors of his hotel suite; he sat that way for a long time.

Hamid al-Issa stood looking out of the window of his apartment; he did not know how to tell his wife that he was leaving, that she could not come with him. A wife and child would be a substantial burden. In addition, taking his family with him would complicate matters for him. It would reveal what he had done and that he had made a mistake that had cost them their future. A man did not tell a woman his business or his mistakes; it is not for women to know.

Hamid stood for a long time watching children at play, birds sailing occasionally past his window. His eyes saw all on the street where he lived, but his thoughts a storm as he struggled for an answer to the rest of his life, there seemed to be no solution, no hope for him.

Then like everyone in desperation, a small solution started to trickle into his thoughts. He could stall; he could lie to his wife that he had a job somewhere. To prevent any alarm, he could tell her that the job was already paying money and that she would be safe, their apartment still their home. Rapidly the force of the idea became stronger, the flavor easier to take than revealing his fatal mistake, after all, he was a very proud man.

That night in bed unable to sleep, Hamid lay on his side facing the window, looking at a moon that was almost full. His thoughts were restless; he looked for an answer in the moon's face, in the way it shone into their bedroom. There was none, just the cold fear of the unknown. He had a plan, but voices still chattered in his head trying to unravel it. Finally, after the moon left him and took its silver light from the bedroom window, he fell into a troubled sleep, his dreams full of prison life.

Roya, Hamid's wife lay awake, she also saw the moon leave. She lay and looked at the form of her husband silhouetted against their bedroom window. Frightened, she needed his arms around her, whispering to her that everything would be well. The karma that had been haunting her, finally came to call, her family had trouble. She could sense very difficult times ahead; they had followed them to America. When they had left their homeland, the future looked so bright. Their apartment was comfortable, they had good food, and she had grown to love it in America. Hamid had told her that he had a job that would take him away for a short period. She knew he was not telling her the truth, he had never been able to hide anything from her, it was a woman's way.

Roya heard her husband's breathing change; he was sleeping. She lay awake for a long time, listening to his heavy breathing.

Alone and lonely, watching the rise and fall of her husband's shoulder, dread slowly invading her heart, Roya knew her comfortable life was over.

CHAPTER - 16

Meetings between Saleem and Carla grew and so did their attraction for each other. Masculine and feminine attractions are very different yet very similar and lead to a common path.

Saleem's emotional conditioning had so many barriers he could not find a way over them or around them.

All he could do was furtively steal a glance at Carla during their frequent business meetings.

Carla's attraction was feminine and also inhibited. Her emotional conditioning also had barriers, she could not be aggressive, this was not way of a woman. In addition, her path leading away from a relationship with a man had many, emotional bruises along the way. She did have the instinct to precipitate a fusion between herself and this very attractive man.

Saleem transferred a substantial amount of money his father promised to an account. He transferred money to Hamid's personal account. Their business would be finished.

Saleem suddenly could see the bridge between them disappearing; he wanted to be with Carla again. The only avenue open was to buy her dinner again and maybe somehow save the bridge.

The last signature was completed, they sat in silence avoiding any eye contact; it was a difficult moment. Carla's phone rang suddenly, it shattered the impasse; she glanced at Saleem, "please excuse me while I take this call." Saleem nodded his head.

When Carla hung up the phone, she glanced up at Saleem, their eyes met. "That was reception, my next appointment is waiting."

Saleem could feel panic rising; this was the end.

Panic is strong, it will not accept many excuses, and it pushed Saleem hard. He took his only option, "You have been very kind, and I appreciate all your efforts, may I buy you dinner again?"

Carla knew they would not see each other again; dinner was a stall and after any possibility of a relationship would be gone.

Suddenly she had an idea, it burst through like the sun dissolving clouds, releasing its brightness.

"I have a better idea, you were very generous, dinner was your gift, and it was an immense pleasure. I would like to compliment you in a similar manner, dinner at my house." Carla had a plan, dinner, soft music, candlelight and but not least, some wine to make things happen.

She sat holding Saleem's eyes captive with hers.

Saleem felt a great surge of release, their path stretched further; hope lay in the distance. "I would like that very much."

All formalities concluded; Saleem left the bank with feeling of elation he had never known in his entire life.

When the doorbell rang, Carla was ready for it. Taking a quick look around she walked toward the door, her movement determined, she knew who would be there. Saleem stood framed in the doorway, very handsome and very masculine. They stood for a moment, struggling with their personal barriers. Finally her heart beating faster, Carla spoke. "Please come in," she said softly.

Childhood conditioning is a powerful barrier, but when Saleem looked at Carla, what he saw is more powerful than the training his culture had instilled. The beautiful woman standing in the doorway captures his eyes; he cannot look away. She is dressed simply but very revealing and he can feel an unfamiliar surge of tension.

The enchanting fragrance she has applied to her body sends teasing wisps at Saleem. Carla steps aside; the way into the apartment is open. Inhaling the fragrance softly, Saleem takes his first step forward and he is inside of her apartment, somehow he knows there is no way back. Lighting is dim; candles strategically placed create an enchanting atmosphere. Saleem stands for a moment, all of it invading him, Carla waiting beside him, "Please come with me," she said in soft voice. Saleem knew in his heart that if he followed the beautiful woman further into her apartment, it would change him forever.

Then a force he does not understand pushes him forward. Slowly he moves further, stepping over the point of no return.

The setting sun lingers, filling the apartment with its golden glow. Saleem pauses, casually glancing around the tastefully furnished room. The sunset, the candles remind him of the restaurant.

Soft music fills the room; it caresses him, soothing some of his nervousness.

"Please make yourself comfortable," Carla's voice is soft and seems to blend with the music. She suggests a sofa against the wall; he slowly eases himself down, again, casually glancing around the room.

Carla's movement stops his visual tour of her apartment; he turns to look at her, she is a beautiful mirage. She is wearing cream-colored slacks, tastefully snug, clinging to her; accenting her buttocks; her long, shapely legs. Guilt prods at Saleem, his culture forbids him to see a woman this way; he cannot stop.

The green, silk blouse blends with Carla's slacks, it is extremely low cut, revealing and clinging to her breasts. Saleem is struggling with his ingrained customs, but he is losing the battle to his eyes, they are too hungry. As she moves, they take him to her round, firm buttocks, the slacks accent the secret places with creases that hold his eyes against his will. Saleem's guilt is overwhelming, but the visual effect of seeing a woman in this manner is also more overwhelming, there seems to be no escape.

Carla knows he is looking at her, it sends a hot surge of excitement through her body. She had prepared for this moment; the loneliness in her life pushed her through barriers she would have not dared before today. Desolate, empty weekends created a hunger that took total control; she could not fight it today. This handsome, elusive man is an overpowering need for her.

This need calls the woman in her; Carla takes her first step in destiny. "Dinner is not quite ready, I have some wine chilled. Would you like to have a glass with me?" The question puts her past the point of no return but somehow today, she does not seem to care.

Saleem hesitates; his answer seems to be taking eternity, Carla stands postured, looking at him, enjoying him, her eyes hungry.

Since he had come to America, he never imagined women were such beautiful creatures. The only women he had ever seen wore a hijab, their shapes a secret, their faces covered. His undiscovered manhood has no mercy today; it pushes him forward. Thoughts flash back to the restaurant and the wine, it had eased his discomfort, brightened colors, the food tasted better, and the evening was soft and enjoyable.

He looks into Carla's eyes, "Yes I will join you." His first step into destiny was exciting.

Carla turns and walks away to prepare their drinks, it is safe to look at her again. Saleem had never imagined a woman walking was so erotic, the rolling movement of her buttocks is a sudden impact that sends his mind back to the elevator and the woman pressing against him. Carla is pouring wine, shifting her weight, her buttocks change shape, and her thighs are full, slim, and erotic.

Saleem suddenly wishes she would hurry with the wine.

Slowly the evening progresses with small talk, the sun loses its power to the candles, Carla's apartment becomes shadowy, mysterious, and the music and wine join hands to soothe the sharp edges of any guilt. Carla's looks are bold and hungry, Saleem looks whenever opportunity will allow, he cannot seem to get enough of her movements, Carla knows he is watching. He cannot seem to get enough of her movements, she knows he is watching and becomes more sensuous. Finally, she knows its time.

Carla sits beside Saleem on the couch, their thighs touching, instantly there is a body heat exchange they both can feel. The evening has softened Carla's perfume, blending it with her body, to Saleem this fragrance is similar to food when one is extremely hungry. It seems like he standing on top of a great height, a new energy pushing him to jump; there is no escape.

For the first time since she made her decision in the shower, Carla is enjoying her newfound freedom. The wine and the evening dissolved any fears she had; she is flying high like a bird. They talk softly, when he looked away, she would steal a look at his midnight black hair, the masculine profile of his face, inhaling the expensive aftershave mixed with his body heat. Carla's feelings flowed through her like a river out of control and abruptly all her restraint ran out like a string, an electric impulse surged through her.

Leaning over Carla kisses Saleem on the cheek, an enticing path lay waiting. "Come with me," she murmurs. Slowly, hesitantly Saleem stands up.

Saleem tries to hesitate but his emotions are in full control, he utters one last, weak refusal, "in my country it is forbidden to touch or look at a woman if she is not your wife."

In full control now, Carla turns and presses her body against Saleem, whispering softly into his ear, "you are not in your country now." Gently, but with insistent strength, she takes his hand and pulls him in the direction of her bedroom, Saleem pulls back slightly then follows the woman into her bedroom.

They stop by Carla's bed; she turns and puts her arms around his neck, pressing against him. Saleem can feel the firm, fullness of her breasts, the nipples are hard pressing into him; they seem like coals of a fire, burning into his chest, it seems to spread throughout his body. Her moist, lips are on his lips, gently caressing, they have a delicious taste, for Saleem this a new flavor he will never forget. The heat from her body is arousing him, suddenly his lips awaken, they seem to know how to accept and blend her searching lips. Carla presses closer, her body demanding his body, searching for arousal. All feminine instincts in her are like a hurricane. Like a great airline, once in the air it reaches a point of no return, it cannot go back to the ground.

Saleem reaches his point of no return, all his conditioning, and barriers crumble, the hunger he still does not understand floods his mind, his body responds. He steps out into the void and can feel the rush of the fall. Gently placing his arms around this sensuous woman, he feels roundness, firmness. At first, his hands are afraid, then slowly they seem to know and drop gently onto her buttocks, his fingers find the secret cleft between them, he pulls Carla closer.

The rest is dreamlike; Carla the aggressor leads Saleem to the top of the mountain and pushes him over. This triggers a long forgotten, female thing within her. It is so strong, almost painful, Carla cannot endure it; she emits a wail of ecstasy. It is gone like a passing whirlwind, she is very tired; contentment spreads through like a warm, comforting flood. Softly she presses against Saleem, her head on his warm chest. Her fatigue calls to the sleep that is waiting, Carla allows herself to sink into the soft, warm void.

Saleem does not move for a long time, enjoying the sleeping woman, feeling her softness against him, her breath warm on his chest, a sweet fragrance rising from her. His culture whispered to him what he did was wrong, but he could not hear, Saleem liked what happened between him and this woman

As he lay holding Carla, somehow it reminds him of when his mother held him, it is not the same.

He cares for this woman in a different way.

CHAPTER - 17

The cell phone tinkled a mystic sound like a silver bell, Mark Jansen reached for the phone clipped to his belt, the call display read Mandy.

Excitement invaded his body like a surge of electricity; he stood looking at the cell phone, its silver bell calling repeatedly. Finally, conditioned reflex took over; he opened the phone and raised it to his ear.

"Hi Mark, how are things?" The voice soft, very feminine, triggered the familiar storm inside of him, it was Mandy Blake a news reporter for a local TV station, his delicious poison. In the past, he had leaked confidential information to her in exchange for what he thought was her attraction to him. Mark discovered too late that she was using him, however his attraction for her was fatal, and she was his addiction. His need for her overcame the terror of discovery and the loss of his job. Today, he knew what she wanted and again this knowledge started the clamor in his head but she always won the battle.

"Things are fine," his voice controlled. The female voice on the cell phone became, softer, more alluring. "We haven't seen each other for a long time, don't you miss me?" Her hook was out, trolling for him.

Mark Jansen had been with the FBI for ten years, he had good focus, attracting attention from his superiors. Promoted to the antiterrorism unit, he never looked back, he like the involvement and detail. The unit was a close group, high motivation making teamwork an inner power. Recently, his work became exciting; terrorism seemed to be lurking everywhere.

Mark had not married, an only child, dominated by his father, his mother a shadow in his life. Searching for a need he did not understand created by the abandonment by his mother, he drifted in and out of relationships. No one seemed to fit his needs, but when someone began drifting closer, his father took the time and energy to eliminate them; Mark slowly began to hide behind his work.

The collision with Amanda Blake was sudden; he did not see her coming. One fatal moment, a very attractive, highly intelligent, predatorial TV newswoman was standing before him. She introduced herself, emphasizing that she liked the name Mandy. She had a developed habit of standing with one hip raised; her hand on that hip, her position turned slightly away, one breast pointing at her victim like a gun. Mandy was all woman and she knew it. While she talked Mandy Blake analyzed him, she could feel her confidence growing; she had created an FBI mole. Focused and energized, she had no one in her life. Occasionally, she would use intimacy to liberate information, it gave her emotional release, and the information she needed to be the star at her job, Mandy Blake loved her work.

Again the soft, alluring voice spoke, "Mark, don't you miss me? It's been such a long time, too long."

Mark avoided the question but memories of their encounters raced through his mind like a speeding car. He got lost in all the flavors of their past encounters.

"Are you there Mark?" The voice was becoming aggressive, demanding, the sharpness of her voice stopped the rush of pictures in his mind. It brought him back to the reality of the moment. Panic that she might hang up brought out his answer. "Yes I miss you." Emotions bombarding him like a hurricane,

Mark stood holding the cell phone to ear, his eyes not seeing the city, or the buildings around him.

"Let's meet for lunch." Mandy's voice became soft and enticing again. "When is good for you?" She used the question as a lever; it focused one's mind to produce the correct answer. Mark's need rose to help control his answer, the sooner the better. He could feel his need for her a pressure, impossible to resist. "Today is good," he said. His heart was beating rapidly; he stood holding the cell phone to his ear, waiting for her answer.

Mandy also could feel the sharpness of her need flow through her, she wanted the story about the office tower downtown, and the FBI would have critical information. "Can we meet at our favorite place?" She murmured softly, and waited breathlessly the reward came suddenly, Mark's voice shattered the silence, and "I will meet you there." Mandy Blake closed the cell phone with a loud snap. "Yes!" She shouted up at the tall spires of Seattle towering over her.

The restaurant sat hidden in an older, downtown area, it had seen Seattle grow up around it. It sat shrunken amidst the tall buildings, a tiny, ancient building with sidewalk tables, delicious pasta kept it from destruction.

During lunch hour the restaurant was a beehive, tables were hard to get once the rush started. Mark came early partially because of the table situation combined with the sharp edges to see Mandy. He sat nursing coffee after coffee, impatiently waiting for her to appear. Finally, his restless and agitated eyes saw her red, sports car race up and expertly park.

His pulse started racing in anticipation, his eyes became riveted to the driver's door. After what seemed eternity, he saw it open and Mandy stood up out of the convertible, sports car. She turned her head, the motion flinging the length of black hair she kept fashionably long like a black tail. She looked back into the car for what seemed a long time, then standing upright and again flinging the black tail, she looked around, her eyes searching, they stopped abruptly at Mark's table. Even at that distance, he could feel her look, for Mark it was like a magnetic shock. She stood there, their eyes locked.

Suddenly without warning, she moved, heading toward his table, her long, shapely legs closing the distance between them rapidly, Mark's eyes feasted on her. She was tall, slim, and shapely; Mandy always wore revealing, slim fitting slacks. They outlined her hips, her long shapely legs. He remembered when she would turn revealing her round, solid buttocks, it would completely unravel him. His eyes traveled over her shape, reaching her breasts. He remembered their firmness against him. Mark liked everything about her. When Mandy Blake came near him, he would become powerless to her demands. Rapidly she walked closer to his table; she smiled spontaneously, revealing perfect white teeth.

Mark sat riveted, just looking. A beautiful woman he could not avoid or deny finally stood at his table.

Mandy stood looking down at him, and then suddenly she bent down and very lightly kissed him on the cheek. Her hair spilled over on his forehead tickling him, the clean, erotic fragrance of her flooded over him. Hunger rose in him, strengthened by the glimpse of her full bosom trying to escape her low-cut top. Mark watched her sit down, his need for her almost painful, her fragrance lingering on his cheek.

All these motions were Mandy's tools and she used them effectively. She sat across from Mark, making direct eye contact. Seconds went by then again she smiled, white teeth flashing, dimples deep and attractive in her cheeks. "Thanks for coming, Mark, I really missed you. Did you miss me?" She sat and waited for his answer, studying the man she had aroused.

Looking away, "you know I missed you Mandy." His response had been slow and when he looked away, Mandy knew her tools were again effective.

Casual chatter started between them, the waiter came, they ordered. People's voices, the clink of dishes surrounded them; the traffic noise on the street became muted by their focus on each other. Mark sat enchanted, absorbing her visually, Mandy sat focused and calculating.

"How are things at work?" Mandy severed the continuous chain of polite chatter. Mark knew what was coming and hesitated, tension suddenly clawing at his shoulders, his answer slow in coming. Finally, looking down at his lunch, he said, "things are okay."

"What is the status on the office tower?" She asked, cutting to the chase.

There it was again.

Mark felt his shoulders bunch up harder, a stiffness climbing up into his neck, he sat looking at his lunch. Without looking up, he said, "Mandy you know I can't discuss that with you."

Mandy was prepared; a plan was solid in her mind. She knew he had trouble saying no to her so she added an additional barrier to a possible, negative answer. "Mark you know that we are good for each other." She waited while he nibbled at his food, looking down at his plate. "Mandy that has nothing to do with anything that is under current investigation, it is confidential, I could get into serious trouble."

"What if I could help you solve the case?" Mandy waited for his answer.

Startled, Mark looked from his lunch, their eyes connecting, "Do you know something I don't." He suddenly felt strong and in control again, his training seemed to have come to the rescue.

She reaches over and places a very soft hand on his, its softness flows through his hand and up his arm, searching for his arousal.

"You know I would never hurt you." Mandy looked directly into Mark's eyes, she knew that is was time to tread carefully. She left her hand on his, maintaining eye contact, radiating sincerity. The softness of her hand reached into his depths, relaxing his barriers.

"What did you have in mind?" He searched her face as if her answer lay hidden in her lips, or her eyes. Memories of their intimacies flickered in his mind; this woman was his total flavor.

Mandy was aware, all her senses working. He did not withdraw his hand, and combined with the question, she was gaining ground. She had to tread carefully now.

"If you had a picture of the person who committed this terrible thing, we could air it on TV. The public would be aware, we would have their traditional sympathy, and the person would have nowhere to hide." She waited, watching him for a response.

Mark's thoughts raced, his training seemed to justify the idea. The idea grew stronger, and then dread started creeping in, disturbing and unsettling the plan. What if his office refused him, they were never strong on media exposure and a media release without authorization severely reprimanded, he could lose his job. On the other hand, if substantial gains occurred, there could be closure for everyone. Mandy would have her story, their relationship would continue, the person or persons responsible for the terrible crime punished. If his actions brought positive results, the premature media release overlooked and he would still have Mandy.

The struggle in his head was subsiding as the idea grew like a bright morning offering promise.

They were still holding hands across the table; Mark reconnected with the sensation and looked up at Mandy. She was beautiful, her hand was soft, a sudden emotion traveled up his arm and into his soul.

"We have a picture of the person who rented the van. If we could question that person, possibly find everyone connected. I could e-mail you the picture." While he talked, Mark kept looking at Mandy, her looks justifying his action, to keep this woman in his life was worth it.

Mandy was soaring; this possibly was the biggest break in her life. This story would take her to heights she could not even imagine. It triggered her imagination and as it took wings, she looked at Mark sitting across the table from her, her eyes did not see him anymore, they saw distant places, exciting things. It was a most exhilarating flight of fancy Mandy Blake had ever experienced in her life. She tingled with the sudden promise of things to happen, her life would change.

Sudden reality brought the flight back to the table, their meeting. She had to ensure this would happen. Her eyes came back to focus, she saw Mark sitting across from her.

"Mark, this could be so good for you and me, I really believe that. After we could meet and celebrate just you and me together, alone." She was careful not to withdraw her hand from his. The impulse was very strong at this moment. Suddenly she was different, not the same Mandy Blake she had been when a few seconds ago. Everything had changed she had changed. Mandy looked at Mark and a new feeling came over her. She needed someone different now. Her life had changed and she had changed. As she sat looking at him, holding her hand, she could see him fading into the distance. Carefully, she withdrew her hand, "I have to go, but promise we will get together again soon.

Standing up, Mandy Blake leaned over and let her hair fall on Mark's face as she touched his cheek with her lips. She knew this was the last time. Turning she walked the same long, legged erotic walk back to her car and her new life.

Mark watched her go, enjoying the fragrance she left behind, the promise of an encounter. She was beautiful and filled his life, leaving no room for anything else. He could feel positive energy; there were things to do to ensure he would see Mandy again.

He beckoned the waiter, paid his bill.

CHAPTER - 18

Hamid sat in his favorite chair, watching the evening news. He had come to a reasonable solution that shut out the chattering voices in his head. Money was coming, a great deal of money, allowing him to leave. Later, he would send for his wife and child. Safety lay waiting.

The newsperson drifted in and out of the bad news of city life, Hamid felt relaxed enjoying the comfort of his home. A pleasant smell of cooking from the kitchen teased his growing hunger. Suddenly the newsperson looked down, hesitated for seconds, and then looked at what seemed directly at Hamid.

"I have just received an update on the inner-city bombing. The FBI just released information that they have a lead, a name of a person involved in the bombing. We will keep you informed as the investigation progresses."

The words penetrated like a sudden, painful jolt of lightening into Hamid's body, his chest contracted, breathing became difficult. Suddenly the thudding of his heart seemed to create energy; he sat up, panic rising like a strong wind. Hamid al Issa sat looking at the flickering television, unable to move then the instinct for flight came to the rescue; he leaped from his comfortable chair and headed for their bedroom.

His wife stopped preparing dinner and stood in their bedroom doorway, she watched while he grabbed a suitcase off a self in the closet. He began throwing handfuls of his clothing into it; his movements were a blur.

Fear drove Hamid's body like an engine with high power fuel. His instinct pushed him to run, where he did not know, reasoning at this moment did not exist, only the instinct to run. Hamid al Issa closed the suitcase, turned and began rapidly walking toward the front door of their apartment.

Hamid's wife Roya, had been watching him all the time, she had heard and seen the flash of news on television. She knew something terrible was wrong and terror rose in her like a silent scream, nausea filled her throat, she was losing her husband. Suddenly, the storm building inside of her broke, a high-pitched wail filled the apartment. Roya ran after Hamid, jumped in front of him, sinking to the floor she threw her arms around his legs and began wailing in the traditional way of women in her country when they lost a child or husband. Finally, she found the strength to ask the terrible question. "What have you done Hamid? Where are you going? What will happen to me?" She sat on the floor holding her husband by the legs, sobbing in with the fear of loss, holding him from leaving. Hamid and his wife stood for seconds, a picture of total sadness, and then he reached down and with some token of gentleness, pulled her arms from around his legs, picked up his suitcase again and moved away from his wife, closer to the door.

"You do not understand woman, I am a soldier for Allah." Hamid, turned, fear of capture pulling at him, he turned and walked out of his present life, closing the door behind him.

Roya heard the final click of the door, the sound releasing a burst of wailing. She sat on the floor, her head down, arms in resigned hopelessness; she knew that somehow her life has changed forever. Roya sat sobbing for a long time, a picture of total despair.

His heart beating rapidly, a suitcase in his hand, Hamid ran down the stairs and out onto the street. As he stepped out of the building, he suddenly felt as if there were eyes watching him. His training and life as a police officer in the Middle East had instilled many impressions in his subconscious mind. An emotional impulse was tugging at him to look around but he forced himself to walk rapidly toward his car parked on the street. Hamid opened the trunk of the car throwing the suitcase inside, walking around to the driver's side; he unlocked the door and got inside. After he started the vehicle, he sat looking down for a long time. Then without looking up at the building where he had lived, his wife watching him from their apartment window, he suddenly pressed on the accelerator and the vehicle surged forward.

Somehow, a feeling tugged at him, this would be the last time he would come back here.

Roya watched the car growing smaller and smaller, she felt as if her soul was leaving her, following the car.

Claws of tension rode his shoulders as he threaded his way through the Seattle streets; The Interstate leading south was his ultimate goal. As he drove, it seemed to Hamid that everyone's eyes were upon him, watching. Every police car he saw made panic dig its claws deeper into his chest and shoulders. Finally, he reached an overpass, a sign stating an exit to the freeway leading south. When he finally entered the highway, Hamid drifted into the extreme right lane, tension seemed to ease inside of him slightly. Blending with the river of cars and trucks, he carefully watched his speed; no rules could be broken to attract attention. Slowly, Hamid eased back into the seat, looking around the countryside, it was spring, and the world was coming alive. The sky, the clouds the gentle rolling hills seemed to tease out a melancholy deep inside of him. Why had his life taken such a drastic turn? He had been so careful, streetwise. All his police training had given him an edge, allowing him to see and predict problems before they happened. As he drove, his life drifted through his mind like pictures. Coming to America had been a good move. It was better here, more opportunities, more money than back home.

When his lifestyle grew better than back home, Hamid began to look around at the lifestyles of Americans, their homes, cars and expensive habits. He wanted to be like them.

Regret came in a sudden rush, almost like nausea; Hamid looked away from the highway rushing at him. Why had he allowed the lure of money Saleem offered? When they had talked, it seemed so good. He could punish his superiors, and have a better lifestyle. It was a simple solution for his needs. A simple mistake had caused his life to crumble like a house of cards.

A surge of guilt rose in him, a sickening feeling; Hamid clenched his fist and hit the steering wheel. He had been so stupid. His driver's license, a simple plastic card had ruined his life. As a police officer, he should have known better. He clenched his fist and hit the steering wheel again.

Suddenly he saw a police car sitting beside the freeway panic shot through him, it was all over.

His car drew closer to the police car, Hamid tensed, watching for the fatal movement. Mind racing, he did not have a plan, the police officer would have a gun, he did not. Besides, if he killed a police officer, there would be no place to hide. Futility slowly overcame his panic; he watched the police car draw nearer, his eyes riveted for any movement. As he drew nearer, he saw the officer looking down at something on the seat of the vehicle, the officer did not look up as Hamid's car drifted past. Heart thumping very hard, Hamid watched the police car grow smaller in his rearview mirror. There was no movement.

Hamid could not believe his good fortune. Elation rose through him like spreading light. It drove away all the sadness and bitter thoughts. Hamid clenched his fist and hit the steering wheel harder, this time it was a feeling of pure joy. Hamid Al-issa drove south toward Mexico with a renewed hope and excitement.

It seemed possible that he could put together the shattered pieces of his life.

CHAPTER - 19

Dinner a distant need, Neil stood on looking out of his living room window, the day slowly ending, leaving behind a red stain on the distant horizon. The sky was slowly deepening into its midnight blue to make a background for the stars.

Neil's melancholy was also deepening, memories of his wife slowly filling him. She was gone, the day was leaving, he stood unable to move, sadness holding him a prisoner.

His cell phone interrupted the flow of melancholy; Neil reached for it and placed it to his ear. The voice was one of his staff, the words rapid, and the voice excited. "Neil, we have a mole in our unit. Someone has released the name and picture of our suspect to a TV station; they are broadcasting everything on the evening news. We will lose the only lead we have for the tower bombing." The excited voice paused, waiting for Neil's response.

His thoughts raced, searching; finally, training came to the rescue. "Send SWAT to the suspect's address and I will meet you there." Neil waited for a response then snapping his cell phone shut, he whirled around, his eyes searching the room for his car keys.

Roya Al-Issa heard the wail of the sirens; she knew they were coming for her husband. Running to the front window of their apartment, she looked out onto the street below. A huge, black vehicle stopped in the middle of the street, it had large white letters on the roof, and sides, the letters read FBI. In addition, on the roof, red lights were flashing.

Suddenly the rear doors opened and men dressed in black began spilling out, they carried automatic rifles. In a tight solid mass, the men began moving toward her building. There was a shout and two men from each side broke away, running toward the sides of the building. The mass of men changed shape, forming a black, human battering ram, moving toward the front entrance. Roya waited, her heart hammering against her chest. They were coming for Hamid but he was safe. Instantly she decided, no matter what they did to her, she would not betray her husband. She felt an impact that shuddered through the building, there was a sound of glass breaking, and the men were inside the building. She knew what was next; her husband had been a police officer. A sound of many heavy feet on the stairs, a moment of silence, then a crash and her door fell into the apartment. The men dressed in black stood looking at her, their rifles pointed at her chest.

One of the men spoke. "Move aside, we are here to search the apartment for Hamid Al-Issa." Roya stood her ground, rifles pointing at her, the men's eyes hard and unmoving.

"He is not here." The sound and strength of her voice surprised her; she could feel strength and resolve flowing through her body. Roya stood her ground, a barrier to the men in the doorway.

The man's voice became softer. "Please move aside, we do not want to harm you, but we must search your apartment." Something in the tone of the voice seemed also to soften the steel of her courage; she looked away. "My child is asleep in the next room, I must get him." Roya turned, walking to her child's bedroom; she heard the rustle of movement as the men rapidly slid along the walls to other parts of the apartment to begin the search for her husband.

Darkness settling on the landscape caught up to Hamid, bright lights started appearing on the other side of the freeway. Hamid had a sudden thought, a small town would be best for what he had in mind. As he drove, Hamid searched for an exit from the freeway. Finally, a sign appeared designating an exit, he slowed, easing his car onto the exit lane leading off the free way.

The hour was late and dinner over, most people had either gone to bed or were watching television, there was no traffic on the side streets. Slowly he drove the street, impatiently looking for the ideal darkened spot; finally, he found one. It was an old neighborhood. Houses were set back on large lots where trees and bushes were overgrown. Streetlights were far apart, and many houses had no lights in the windows. There was a car parked beside some high, dense bushes, they would hide his car from the owner's house. Slowing his car down to a crawl, Hamid switched off his headlights, stopping directly behind the other car. The streetlight quite a distance down the block, made the area dark. Hamid rolled down the window and sat quietly, his eyes searching for signs of human activity. Wanting to be sure, he sat this way for long minutes.

Finally, he looked in the glove box for a screwdriver and found nothing. A sense of panic started to rise, he sat for a moment, thinking and fighting the panic. A thought struck him; there could be something in the trunk of his car. Sometimes he kept tools there for emergencies. He opened his door and the old, worn hinge betrayed him, it emitted a loud creak. Down the street, a dog started barking furiously. Hamid sat very still, fighting the stress that was threatening him. Suddenly there was a shout and the dog stopped barking, somewhere, a door slammed shut and silence cloaked the area again. Hamid did not move his door again. He eased out his car and walking around to the back, opened the trunk; it was dark inside. Even if he had a flashlight, he would not have dared to risk it. Bending down, He began groping around for tools. He could not remember leaving any, his mind raced and he reached further into the blackness of the trunk, there was nothing anywhere. He stood up thinking, rising panic threatening him again. There was something sticky on his fingers from the trunk. Instinctively, he rubbed his fingers on the side of his trousers; he could feel coins in his pocket. Elation raced through him, they were the answer, and he would use a larger coin to remove the screws on the plates of the car. Reaching into his pocket, he took out the largest coin. He walked to the space between the two vehicles. Squatting down into the darkness, he began groping around like a blind man, searching for the plate and the screws holding it.

Luck came to his rescue finally; the car was old and neglected. There were only two screws holding the plate secured to the bumper. They were loose and came out easily; he held the stolen plate to his chest, heart thumping against it. The front plate was easier, there was only one screw holding it in place, he removed it. Walking back to his car, he stood for a moment beside the open door, and then he slid into the driver's seat and reached for the door to close it. The hinge had been waiting for this moment to betray him. There was a loud creak, another dog started barking furiously again. Hamid slammed the offending door, started his car, and then drove down street, his lights turned off. It was too late for anyone to catch him now, besides if anyone came out onto the street, in the darkness, darkness would hide the missing plates. Two blocks away, he turned, turned on his headlights, and then headed back toward the entrance to the freeway.

He glanced at the stolen license plates on the seat beside him. A thought suddenly came to him, there would be service stations open into the late hours, and they would have tools he could buy. The entrance to the freeway suddenly loomed in front of him and he eased into the circle that took him back, heading south.

Hamid's thoughts soared, he was safe, and soon he would be free in Mexico to pursue the rest of his plans. He leaned back into the seat, relaxing his body, his eyes searching the dark countryside for the lights of a service station.

It was midnight when Neil's unit had their emergency meeting. Everyone stood in a group, their eyes wide with curiosity, and an expectant air in the room. Neil stood in front of the group, looking down at the floor for what seemed an eternity. Nervous energy started a rustle among them. Someone coughed, a cell phone tinkled, the person did not take the call. They all stood looking at Neil, waiting.

"One of us is a mole." Neil's words were sudden and his voice hard. He stood looking at the group of agents, waiting to see the impact his words had caused. Their eyes widened, there were gasps and noises of feet shuffling. It was as if a sudden gust of wind hit a tree, shaking the leaves, causing motion and sound.

Everyone eyes were on Neil, waiting for him to continue, one man looked away. This was the impact Neil had been waiting for; the mole revealed himself.

"Someone released secure information to the media, a picture, and the name of our   suspect in the tower bombing; he probably saw the evening news and left in a hurry. SWAT arrived at the suspect's address too late. At this point, we have no one, except our mole. Does anyone have suggestions how to proceed?" Neil stood looking at the group; his words had hit them hard. Some were talking rapidly to each other; others stood looking at Neil, their eyes wider now. Voices became louder and louder. Neil's eyes were on one person that stood looking down at the floor in silence. According to his file, he was a good agent, dedicated and focused. Would it serve a purpose to rid the unit of his positive energy? After all, everyone makes mistakes. The answer came to him.

"Can I have your attention?" Neil raised his voice to overcome the voices in the room. Their chatter continued. "Please everyone." His voice was almost a shout. Suddenly there was silence; everyone stood looking at him, even the mole.

"If we spend our energy looking for the person among you who destroyed our only lead, the suspect will have time to run further. Don't you all agree?" The unit stood looking at him; no sound came from them. "The person among you, who released vital information, had personal reasons, but we don't have time to try and understand motives. We have a suspect to catch. This will never happen again. Should something of this nature occur again, the person responsible will lose their job and possibly wind up with a criminal record." No sound came from the group gathered in the room. The offender stood looking at Neil, there seemed to be gratitude shining in his eyes.

"We have a license plate number for the suspect's car; issue an interstate alert to all police agencies and our offices, let's move." His words released them and they scattered in personal directions. Neil stood watching them leave. They were a good group.

Hamid Al-Issa drove carefully to the Mexican border, obeying all the rules, watching relentlessly for police cars. He was flying high, he would be safe, have his family and life back when he got there. Today would be a good day.

CHAPTER - 20

W hen the boy was very young, drinking problems followed his father home, forcing his mother also to haunt bars, searching for happiness.

He evolved directionless, positive values were always out of reach on the distant horizon. Sitting alone in his room, unhappy and abandoned he would dream of ways to put his sad and painful emotions to rest. Friends drifted in and out his life causing additional pain to his burden.

The boy grew up looking for the path that would lead him away from his agony.

He joined the army only to find authority difficult, superiors were harsh, demanding, often exploding into anger tirades like both his parents. His anger grew, fed constantly by a belief the world was a cruel and unjust place.

Gunnery training provided by the armed forces revealed a sliver of personal satisfaction; he withdrew into the world he liked best, shooting things.

Entering the war, the war, excitement flowed through him like a river. The chaos of killing and war gave him some personal closure, it helped feed his anger, and ease part of the burden he carried, Andy Bierkow could channel his hurts to others. Further peace surfaced when he met some extremists in

Iraq. The extremists were not like others in his past; they were loyal and did not leave him. For the first time in his life he drew closer, feeding a need that been hidden deep inside of him. It was a simple task to convince him that America was cruel and wrong. They convinced him that killing is indeed wrong, but in order to help many, one must hurt a few, that is Allah's way. If he would be a soldier for Allah, he could be a true soldier with a just cause. For the first time in his life, he could feel a new energy filling him, a loyalty to his new friends and their beliefs.

Back in America, he drifted from job to job, relationship to relationship. Nothing lasted, he found his parents flaws in everything and everyone, and unhappiness trailed him like a black shadow. A cheap apartment his only haven, he lay in bed alone staring at the cloud patterns in the sky seeing only sadness in the colors and tones, wondering where he belonged. His parents finally separated into different paths, he had no brothers or sisters, any family, he was alone in the world, and sometimes the sadness seemed to want to crush him.

One day, in between jobs, the last few dollars the only financial security in his world, a man phoned him. He said he was a friend with his friends in the Middle East. The man's voice and tone were mild and persuasive. They met in a park and talked Saleem Dal Figar promised his a great deal of money if he would be a soldier for Allah. The heavy burden of his financial and emotional needs lifted, he agreed with enthusiasm.

That night he could not sleep, excitement blocked it. Images of freedom and closure danced in his head like a movie. The black shadow of sadness lay forgotten somewhere behind. For the first time in his life, Andy Bierkow had direction; he could see the path leading off into closure and happiness.

Getting is final clearance, the plane suddenly leaped forward, racing down the runway, the blue-sky open, and waiting. Inside the cockpit, Seattle Tower chatted with the pilot, who in turn gave standard instructions to the copilot. The take off was working like a well-oiled machine, almost nudging at the forbidden area of boredom.

Its wing flaps dropped and the plane rose like a great bird, the ground rapidly falling away. Tucking the wheels into its belly, the huge plane rose into the freedom of the sky, sunlight glinting off its windows as it turned in response to the pilot's commands inside its cockpit.

Tim Olson finally sat deeper into his seat, Seattle Tower still chattering at him. Occasionally he confirmed necessary information. The take off was very routine and his mind drifted to other things in his life. He and his wife had purchased a new house on the outskirts of the busy, noisy city. It was a new home in a new housing project; it bordered the open fields that stretched for miles like a green carpet. Excitement tingled throughout him and he looked of the cockpit window on his left side, he could see the solitary, blue mountain rising out of the green landscape. In the mornings and evenings, his bedroom window was a picture frame for the mountain. Through the cockpit window, he looked at the white swirls of cloud patterns in the blue sky. His life was in order; a bright happy future lay in the distant horizon. A conditioned reflex made Tim lean forward and the press the button to allow the passengers to unfasten their seat beats.

Shirley West saw the seat belt sign go out, it was her signal to start her organized schedule of preparing the in-flight drinks and meal for her passengers. The routine was also conditioned reflex, allowing her mind to wander, traveling again to her spots of unhappiness. There was still no one of significance in her life; anyone she met was short-lived, leaving behind spots of sadness that would gather to haunt her. She took a deep breath and focused on her work. This was the signal for the spots to withdraw, to wait for another opportunity. Temporarily free, Shirley began her repetitive routine in the galley. The work made her feel good; her job was really all she had. As she got deeper into her routine, she could feel a new energy start to flow.

A solitary figure sat on the lonely shore of the Pacific Ocean, some miles south from the Seattle airport. The man kept glancing northward along the seacoast, beside him on the sand lay a rocket launcher; armed and ready

He had chosen the spot well; the shore was rocky, offering spots of seclusion, place where he could hide from any detection. In addition, along this rocky coastline, there were pools along the rocks, some deep and dark, places where he could dispose of the rocket launcher.

Andy Bierkow was restless, constantly, looking northward. He could not see the blue sky, the soft clouds, the restless, blue ocean stretching west to bond with the sky. His eyes were blind to everything except a dark spot that would appear on the northern horizon. He felt restless, energy flowing through him like caged electricity, looking for an opening to escape. There was no turning back, he had taken the money, promised friends, the path to his yesterdays had disappeared forever.

Andy stood up and stretched, stiff from sitting on the rock. His eyes seemed to control him, they turned his head northward again, and there was still nothing in the sky.

He had checked flight schedules days before, today the energy pushed him, controlled him with its pressure. Andy glanced at his watch it would be soon. His eyes took him north again, still nothing. Looking down at the rocket launcher, he checked it visually everything was ready. He seemed to feel his pulse in his temples, his chest, and his arms. A seagull landed on the shore nearby and suddenly screamed startling him; he looked at the bird strutting arrogantly on the sand near the water. The bird looked back at him defiantly, its look constant. Andy could feel irritation flow through him. The gull continued to stare and Andy picked up a stone, hurling it at the bird. For a split second, the gull hesitated, and then with another annoying scream, its wings spreading, the gull leaped into the air, protesting with more screams. Finally, it disappeared along the southern shoreline; the sudden silence soothing, Andy looked north again.

His heart leaped against his chest, there was a speck in the distance. Because of the distance, it did not resemble an airplane but Andy Bierkow knew it was time. He knelt down beside the rocket launcher, checking and rechecking anxiety a powerful pressure pounding inside of him. Without looking up, he could hear the distant whistle of jet engines. He was ready; everything was going according to plan. He had the money, the rocket launcher would be at the bottom of a deep pool in the ocean, and he would be free for the first time in his life.

Inserting the rocket into the tube of the launcher, he placed it on his shoulder and squatted down in the sand, again, his eyes took control he looked northward. The speck had become a plane, the jet engines whistling louder. As he watched, the shape began to change; wings seemed to grow out of the shape, engines hanging from them. The sun glinted on the window on the pilot's windshield. The jet's engines whistled louder, building the pressure inside of him. Andy Bierkow squatted on the sand, suspended in time, his eyes fixed on the approaching plane.

A roar replaced the whistle of the jet's engines as it approached the shoreline where Andy knelt on the sand, the rocket launcher on his shoulder. Finally, the right wing dropped, the plane began its turn toward the southwest, exposing it tail, and the holes of its engine exhaust, distorted by the heat rushing from them. Andy had been waiting for this moment.

A red eye winked suddenly in the launcher, the rocket awoke, aware of its purpose. It sensed the heated air from the jet's engines exhaust. The red eye watched, waiting for release.

The huge, silver plane was still below 11,000 feet, its exhausts radiating a huge field of heated air.

It was time, Andy lined up the rocket launcher and pulled the trigger, the rocket responded like a trained hawk.

Smoke trailing like a white, rope tethered to earth, and the missile leaped at the receding plane, following it, narrowing the distance. The red eye was accurate, like a living predator, it adjusted constantly to the plane's changing direction. Without warning, an object suddenly parted from the missile, it had discarded its launch engine, its fuel gone. Without a pause, a second rocket engine obediently lit, the missile never wavered, its red eye kept blinking hungry for the searing heat inside a jet engine. Reaching the exhaust hole of an engine hanging from the left wing, the missile disappeared into the opening. Microseconds elapsed before the red flower of the explosion appeared from the huge plane, its petals tinged with black. Pieces of engine, began raining to earth, the wing cut in half followed, twisting, and turning in the tortured air. The delicate balance of the plane changed, weight of the other wing and engine pulled down, the plane rolled on its right side, starting its fatal drop to ocean waiting below.

A sudden, shuddering explosion abruptly turned off the images of green fields and the blue mountain, Tim Olson looked left out of his window. He could not believe his eyes, red flame, and black smoke were reaching toward him like fingers. The left engine had exploded. He had only a split second to see the empty space where the wing had been, when the plane rolled onto its right side. Trained instincts took over his body, he fought for control but the plane was doomed, it did not belong in the sky anymore. He sat in terror, watching the ocean getting closer. His mind racing, he found one sad thought before the plane's nose entered the water, shattering the windshield, cold water hitting him, killing him. Tim Olson had a perfect image of his wife; his last thought was how he loved her.

Shirley West fell backwards in the aisle, the trolley she had been pushing to service breakfast slammed into the forward bulkhead, she did not understand. For seconds, she lay looking at the ceiling of the plane, and then terrified passengers started screaming. The sound increased until it became solid sound, almost painful to her ears. Then something stronger took over, her sadness. Shirley West knew she was going to die, Shirley had last thoughts of how her life could have been better; she wished she could have known true love.

The plane hit the serene, blue Pacific Ocean, entering rapidly, leaving behind a plume of water that rose in the air, and then it fell back, following the plane. The ocean had known many disruptions; it closed around the plume, leaving only a giant bubble, and finally a whirlpool. Slowly the waters settled, closing the wound, there was no debris on the surface, it was as if nothing had happened this blue pacific morning.

Andy Bierkow stood looking out to sea, the violent tragedy he created, had disappeared into the ocean. There was nothing, only gulls wheeling and calling, the blue sky looked serene, peaceful; the ocean resembled a sheet of blue glass stretching into infinity. A peaceful scene of solitude surrounded him.

His feelings became a storm, guilt, and remorse battered at his thoughts. Andy fought back, aided by the fact there were no carnage or bodies, only silence. His thoughts went to the money waiting for him. Excitement overwhelmed any remorse, he could do many things, buy many things; his life had changed.

Andy Bierkow turned and started walking south along the shore of the ocean. There was a rocky cliff in the distance. There would be a deep pool, an ideal place to sink the rock launcher forever. No one would find it, he would disappear, no one would know.

CHAPTER - 21

Neil could not believe what he was hearing, a passenger plane leaving Seattle airport went down into the Pacific Ocean. Could this be another act of terrorism while a suspected terrorist was still loose? Neil doubted that the suspect committed the second act; he was too high a profile.

The morning brought chaos into his office; he had to assemble a new unit to investigate the horrific event. There were no leads; the only information from the airport traffic tower revealed the plane suddenly disappeared from the radar scan. The ocean would be a difficult place to retrieve clues. Divers would have to find the wreck, possibly in very deep water. Once found, only special salvage equipment could bring the plane to the surface, it would be full of bodies.

Neil sat at his desk, mentally sorting the pieces of this new tragedy, combined with the bombing of the office tower, the pressure he felt was tremendous. It seemed to be a terrible dream, the only light at the end of this black tunnel was to wake up, Ellen would still be there beside him, life was happy. Abruptly, his cell phone interrupted, bursting his thoughts like a bubble. Under his orders, a new unit was ready, but had no direction. Neil's mind raced while the caller waited patiently. An idea suddenly flashed like a flight of startled birds leaving a tree. Was it pilot error, a bomb on board, someone killing the pilot, or someone targeting the plane from land?

Information from the radar tower confirmed the plane had just taken off, climbing into a turn. Could it have been someone from the ground?

"We will start from the airport, along the ocean shore. There could be clues of someone shooting at the plane. I will meet you downstairs." Snapping the phone shut, he rapidly, headed downstairs to start the hunt.

The search became tedious, the unit encountered beachcombers, their dogs running free, some barking at the unit members, irritating them. There were overnighters, still sitting on their sleeping bags, staring at the unit. Further, down the beach, there were people searching for seclusion, they sat on logs, special canvas chairs, or just meandered along the beach. The shoreline had been totally contaminated, it seemed useless to look for clues of any kind. Slowly they worked the shoreline, discouragement settling heavily on everyone.

It was past dinner and everyone was tired, hungry, disenchanted, there had been no clues and no reward. They stood on a now deserted shoreline, it stretched south, seemingly endless. The only sound was the tide returning, the routine of the sea.

Looking southwest at the endless ocean, Neil frantically searched for a reason to continue and it came, like a flash in his mind.

Why would there be clues in the busiest part of the shoreline? A terrorist is secretive, not wanting discovery. It did not make sense to search a heavily populated area, he looked south at the sand stretching endlessly. Fatigue persistently nagged at him, he could feel the group's eyes on him, wanting the correct answer. Neil stood looking south, feeling the pressure of his idea and the members penetrating eyes. A long way down there was a rocky formation that ran down an embankment and disappeared into the ocean. He looked at the unit members, "See that rock formation, I would like us to go there." He stood his arm outstretched; pointing at the distant rock formation, the group emitted groans and mumbled phrases. The group knew him, trusted him, many times his hunches had been correct. A voice said, "We should do it." Neil recognized the voice, it belonged to the mole, he turned his head to look at the unit; the mole met his eyes with a confident look, he had asked to be included in the new unit to prove his loyalty.

The group emitted more murmurs and groans but they were a cohesive unit. Suddenly as one, they all turned, heading toward the rocky formation a long way down the deserted shoreline.

They found only rocks, empty clamshells and logs that had lain there for ages. Hope faded, adding more weight to their leaden feet. Suddenly someone shouted, "I found something!" Everyone felt the surge of adrenalin and rushed to the spot.

Someone had been there, waiting on the desolate shoreline. There were footprints in the sand and cigarette butts beside a curious depression in the sand. Footprints were leading away from it toward the rocky formation. Neil stood looking at it. There seemed to be something that been laying in the sand, it had the shape of a long pipe.

The mole took the initiative, he walked slightly away from the tight group, stood for a minute and then he knelt down in the sand. Everyone stood watching and waiting. Standing up carefully, not to disturb an impression he found, the mole stepped away from a shape in the sand exactly like the one they found earlier.

Neil looked at the long tubular depression and he knew instantly, a rocket launcher. This was where the terrorist had waited to shoot down the plane full of people. He looked further down the beach, the rocks and the ocean held the rest of the secret in the deep pool. He turned his head around to survey the surrounding countryside, a neglected, old road ended at the shoreline. Someone had easy access to this deserted spot.

"Pick up the cigarette butts for DNA and then let's go home to have a good dinner and relax. You are all a good group," again as one, they all turned heading the long way back to their vehicles, their steps were lighter, and their laughter sparkled in the air.

For Neil, that evening, even the prospect of an empty house seemed not as ominous. In the morning he would issue a complete description of Hamid al-Issa's car, the police could not seem to find him with an APB on his license plate.

While Carla Black made her dinner, the fragrances from the cooking food were like Aromatherapy, it reminded her when she cooked dinner for Salem. Carla drifted through her evening routine, savoring her beautiful memories, tingling through her; it had been a long time since she had been with a man, his arms around her. Carla could still feel their pressure, arousal started as she went back to each delicious moment. Their first kiss, he resisted, she had to soften his lips with hers, and arousal came to her like a hot tide. She remembered how she had felt his arousal and taken him softly, slowly to the delicious, explosive sequence. For her, the explosive closure had been unbelievable. Suddenly, she stopped setting the table and walked to the window, the room seemed hot.

An emotionally agitated voice in background interrupted her delicious memory trip. It was the evening news on TV. She hated the news, whether in the newspaper, radio or television, it brought more imperfection to an imperfect world, giving an impression life was a useless struggle. She hated being alone more, the television kept her company.

It was something about a passenger plane leaving Seattle airport and falling into the ocean. Carla walked into the living room and stood watching the news anchor, he was very emotional, his eyes wide, his voice growing louder, "All the people in the plane were lost, it seems there is terrorism in America?" The man on TV took a deep breath to regain control; a picture of Hamid al-Issa flashed on the screen, Carla did not recognize him. Slowly she ate her lonely dinner; evening settled in, shadows came out of hiding. Starting the lonely cleanup of dishes, something kept troubling her; she searched her thoughts and found nothing. Carla continued the clean up but the feeling would not leave her. She shook her head to clear it, deciding she would read for a while before bed.

The TV news combined with other subliminal memories joined hands and jumbled her dreams, making a confusion of images and memories. A tiny hidden recollection of Hamid al - Issa's picture on TV burst her dreams like a bubble and Carla sat upright in bed. Something kept tugging at her, she struggled, and searching until fatigue won the battle, dropping her back into a troubled sleep. In the morning, tired and irritable Carla jumped into the shower, had breakfast on the run, leaving the dishes in the sink. A dark, foreboding feeling kept tugging at her, insistent, unrelenting. Carla turned on the car radio, searching for some soft music; bad news lurked everywhere, she turned it off. Morning traffic was exceptionally slow; her commute seemed to take forever. Finally arriving at her office, she gave quick nods to co-workers and hurried to her office. An unsettled feeling trailed behind her like a black shadow; she could not shake the feeling.

Midmorning, the emotional weight became unbearable, after coffee, Carla decided to do a computer search. Typing in some information, she waited, the computer seemed exceptionally slow, suddenly the monitor flashed with information. Tightness filled her chest when she found the money transfer to a Hamid al-Issa from Saleem. Carla could not believe her eyes, her world collapsed; she pivoted around in her chair and sat looking out of the office window. Her troubled eyes could not see the blue sky, the fluffy clouds. Sadness and fear settled on her like a suffocating weight, the day became the longest day of her life. Co-workers drifted in and out like shadows, her hands and body obeyed routine, her mind was a storm.

During the evening commute, Carla could not really see or hear the traffic; her trained reflexes took her home safely to the lonely apartment. She tried making a small meal, but hunger had deserted her. Completely preoccupied she accidentally dropped cutlery into the sink creating loud irritating noises. Finally, Carla left her dinner uneaten, sitting on the kitchen counter.

Unable to sleep, Carla lay staring at the window defined by outside light, her eyes wide, not seeing anything, her life from her failed marriage to the intimate relationship with Saleem, seemed a long black, hopeless tunnel. Now the recent, delicious memories turned ugly, she had gone to bed with a possible killer. A shudder passed through her, Carla turned on her side away from the thoughts, but they stayed with her, chattering until morning.

Carla Black had to find an escape from this nightmare.

CHAPTER – 22

Neil's office bordered on chaos; there were two acts of terrorism to deal with. The file on the first case was still open, going nowhere. He tried to focus on priorities.

There were still no results from the APB on Hamid's vehicle. Suddenly a thought crossed his mind; the police would only stop anyone with the correct license number.

Neil picked up the telephone, his mind racing. Mexico was the logical gate for anyone running, the authorities at the border would be looking for the license plate numbers. He had to issue an APB on the description of the vehicle.

Elated, Hamid al-Issa continued toward Mexico and safety. On several occasions, police cars had pulled in behind him, checked his license plate and then passed him at high speed. His police training had saved him.

It was after midnight when he reached the Mexican border traffic was almost nonexistent.

His car was a solitary vehicle in the lane to the glass booth, on the other side lay safety.

A uniformed Mexican guard stood waiting. Suddenly the man went inside, reappearing seconds later. Uniformed border guards began pouring out of a larger building; automatic rifles positioned with the butt on their hips. The guard was waving his arms, signalling Hamid to stop, not to approach the booth.

Hamid knew instantly, it was a flash of sudden heat through his body, his face, tingling in his arms. Once they stopped him, it would be over.

His decision came suddenly. Hamid backed his car about 120 feet from the glass booth, and then he stopped. He sat there, the border guards confused but alert, watching. His thoughts about his life, his wife, and child, a river full of sadness through his mind. Hamid knew in his mind, he could not go back, face humiliation, prison. What he had done was just in his mind, no one else would understand. From his police years, Hamid knew he could not serve a sentence, live in prison. He reached for the lever on the steering column and put it into drive. Hamid took a moment more and then he drew a deep breath, stepped hard on the gas pedal, his car roared to life, leaping forward. Hamid al-Issa was living his last moments. There was money arranged for his family and once he entered paradise, he would be safe forever.

The Mexican border guards saw him coming, the attendant who summoned them, began waving his arms, the guards brought their weapons up. Their officer waved his arms harder but Hamid did not slow down.

When the first star appeared on his windshield, Hamid was emotionally ready, it seemed as if he was in a dream, floating. The bullets began hitting the windshield rapidly; making more stars, popping everywhere until he could not see the guards shooting at him. Suddenly a hot poker hit him in the shoulder, burning, forcing its way through him, then another in his other shoulder, it was as if red-hot rods penetrated his body. The final impact came as an explosion in his head. There was no pain; just an incredible pressure, a burning and Hamid knew he was entering paradise. There was no time for last thoughts or sadness. He stiffened his leg pressing the accelerator to the floor, the car roared forward, slamming into the protective, concrete barriers. Its front end crumpled backward into the engine, stalling it. There was silence as the Mexican border guards stood in shocked silence. Hamid al-Issa slumped forward, lifeless.

Roya leaped up in bed, a sound, a shout, something had wakened her from the restless sleep, she looked at Hamid's place it was empty; the bedroom filled only with shadows and silence. Something had wakened her, she listened for sounds from her son's bedroom, nothing. A sadness she could not understand seemed to settle on her like a heavy weight. Roya sat upright in the partial darkness of the bedroom for a long time, and then she lay down, facing the light in the window. She did not sleep until morning.

Abandoned by her appetite, dinner a distant thought, alone in her apartment, Carla felt trapped. She avoided the news on TV now that it seemed to involve her and did not turn the television on until she had poured herself a glass of wine. Taking several deep sips, Carla could feel it flow through her; the sharp edges of anxiety seemed to withdraw. Glancing at the TV, she hesitated, then slowly walked over, picked up the remote turning the set on. The local news burst onto the screen, the news anchor still emotional, he talked as if Seattle and the world were in chaos. Anxiety started returning, Carla turned off the television and poured herself another glass of white wine. She sat looking at the sky changing color, looking for an answer in the clouds. Sipping wine, she struggled with disgust trying to overwhelm the delicious memories of the sensuous moments with Saleem. Carla won the struggle temporarily; she finished the bottle of wine and fell asleep in the armchair, her head tilted to the side. The sun disappeared, leaving her hidden in a shadow, temporarily safe from her emotional storm.

Andy Bierkow awoke early; he stood in his one room apartment and looked around at the dismal surroundings. An unmade cot he slept on, fast food containers on the counter of the tiny kitchenette, creased shirts and trousers, unwashed and worn many times, lay around on the few chairs. The small room had a tiny window that permitted very little light, adding to depressing karma. He took a deep breath then turned and walked toward the door, he was leaving this place for the last time. He had money, a great deal of money. Waiting on the distant horizon would be an apartment with a view, a new car and new clothes. His world had changed overnight, everything had become exciting and a bright future lay ahead. Andy slammed the door shut, heading for the bright sunlight outdoors and his new, exciting life.

Neil received the information about the incident at the Mexican border, something was wrong. The suspect in the office tower bombing was dead, the case officially closed, but something would not rest in his mind. Could one security guard plan and execute such a plan as the office tower bombing? Were there more people involved? He looked over the file on Hamid al-Issa; the man was an ex-police officer, worked as a security guard and lived in low-income area. He had a wife and child. Was there enough reason for him to plan such a massive, destructive kill? He looked over his notes on the interview with Hamid's supervisor. Apparently, Hamid had spoken out about America, its ways. Because of his attitude, he lost the promotion to supervisor. Would that be enough anger to kill?

Neil sat and looked out of the window in his office, his eyes not seeing the city outside, his thoughts searching.

A knock on the door of his office brought him back suddenly, it was a lab technician and she had information about the DNA from the cigarette butts found in the sand on the shoreline south of the Seattle airport.

The technician sat in a chair across from Neil and handed him a file. She spoke, "we found the person belonging to the DNA," her soft voice very feminine. She was careful with authority, waiting for Neil to be first with the information in the file. Her soft, voice triggered something and he looked up at her, she was a pretty woman. It triggered memories of his wife, how deeply he missed her. Neil took a deep breath, sat forward in his chair opening the file.

The young woman stood up, "I leave you with results." She turned and walked out of the office, closing the door with a soft click.

Neil watched her go; she left behind the soft sound of her voice; her fragrance and her gentle woman's way. All of it again brought his wife's face back and memories flickered like a movie. Neil struggled, and then with a shake of his head and another deeper breath, he opened the file to read the results of the DNA.

Results referenced a GI in the forces. Neil's thoughts wandered back to the beach, he could see the spot again. Cigarette butts were beside the telltale impressions in the sand. Looking over the service record of the man, he saw that he had specialized in rocket launchers. This information teased at his thoughts, he leaned forward and picked up the telephone, keyed in a select number then issued instructions for an APB on Andy Bierkow.

Hamid was gone, leaving no trail back, the plane full of people shot down over the ocean, also would leave no clues. Both acts would certainly get the Americans attention.

For the first time in his life, Saleem dal-Figar felt a personal glow of pride, his self-esteem reinforced, he felt good about himself. Taking a deep breath, Saleem, reached for the remote and turned off the television. Energy pushed at him, like wind in a sail. He stood up and walked around his penthouse, his mind searching, suddenly a thought flashed, he needed a reward for his accomplishments; the reward should be Carla Black.

Images and sensations came flooding back. He could see her again, the shape of her, the curves of her body, the way her clothing clung to her body, revealing more when she moved or walked. Arousal caused him to take a deep breath; he could smell her fragrance, then the woman smell when they were intimate. His need took control, pushing him, his emotional voices urging. Saleem walked to the telephone and keyed in Carla's number, impatiently he waited, edgy, restless. The phone seemed to ring forever, on and on, finally Carla answered, her voice without emotion. After the "hello," she did not speak; there was silence on the telephone between them. His need was insistent, it pushed and Saleem could feel its force. He spoke of dinner, the excellent menu and the two of them at his hotel. Saleem suggested he would pick her up, asking about a time convenient for her, still, only, silence from her end. Then Carla spoke, her voice cold, "I don't think I can make it." The silence between them solid, Carla being his first woman, Saleem did not have the experience to coax her. Suddenly there was buzzing, Carla had hung up. Saleem stood there, pressing the phone to his ear, the buzzing loud in his ear; finally he bent over and hung up the telephone.

Shattered, he stood and looked into the distance, confused by the emotions storming through him.

His recent accomplishments came to the rescue; they were still a powerful force inside of him. Saleem dal-Figaar shrugged off the rejection and decided to have dinner alone the menu was excellent. Downstairs, there would be American women walking around, their clothes very revealing. He could feel the flavour that he would never be able to resist. On the way down in the elevator, Saleem decided he would have a glass of wine, he liked where it took him. He would have dinner and look around for attractive women.

After she hung up the telephone, Carla stood looking at it for a long time. From her call display she had known it was Saleem calling, she hesitated answering, but experiences in her marriage revealed it just prolonged the stress.

Abruptly, she turned and sat in her favourite chair. Her lips compressed into a thin line, her hand clenched in her lap, Carla Black sat looking out of the window in silent desperation.

Her marriage had been a sentence of hardship with a controlling, abusive husband. Carla suddenly walked out and never went back.

Now she was in a situation again, attracted to a handsome client, she broke the rules and slept with him. She was his first woman and Carla had never experienced anyone like that in her life. He was very masculine, hesitant and finally submissive. Carla sat looking at the sky and the clouds, the memories teasing her; she could feel the heat of arousal seeping into her body.

Abruptly, the thought came like a painful, electric shock, shattering soft memories into fragments; she had slept with someone who was killing people, a terrorist. Nausea rose, her knuckles turned white as she clenched her hands, felt sickened, ashamed, remorse settled on her like an unbearable weight. Carla Black sat in the armchair in silent desperation for a long time, her values an emotional storm.

Slowly shadows deepened around her, darkening her apartment. Carla sat facing the light in the window, a glow on her features. Finally as if coming out a coma, her chest rose as Carla inhaled deeply, she sat for a few seconds more then stood up and walked over to the telephone, she stood and looked at it for what seemed eternity. Carla Black was fighting an emotional battle; her values were the deciding factor.

She picked up the telephone, took another deep breath and keyed in the number written on a piece of paper, the police answered.

CHAPTER - 23

The police found Andy Bierkow's car outside an automobile dealership, their orders were to "stand down" and call the FBI. The police car pulled around a corner to reduce detection and waited, watching for the suspect to exit.

Neil received the call and immediately assembled the Tactical Team, informing the captain he would be on the scene and not to use sirens, they were to assemble near the dealership, outside the perimeter of detection and wait for his instructions.

Andy Bierkow stood in the showroom looking at the glistening new vehicles; a strange, new excitement was pounding in his temples, tingling in his arms, a pressure in his body. He had never been so close to a new car, they had always been financially out of reach, a hope somewhere on the distant horizon. He inhaled the smell of leather, the strong aroma of new rubber of the tires, a total fragrance of a strange, new pleasure.

When Neil arrived at the auto dealership, the police and the FBI surrounded the building without revealing their presence. Neil had been feeling such immense pressure from all the recent events, he felt it could only be relieved if he was more inside the loop. Procedure required a bulletproof vest; it felt strange and bulky, restricting his movements. Checking his weapon, he placed it back in its holster and looked at the dealership. Tension began building; he could feel it stiffening his body, its claws digging into his shoulders. Neil had parked across the street from the dealership, his unmarked car, unnoticeable, just another car on the street. Neil sat and looked through the glass front of the building. Customers were apparently scarce at this time, was no one in the showroom, a good thing for the impending action.

He felt himself stiffening more as his mind prepared his body for the familiar "let's do it" trigger. The moment arrived like a bubble bursting; he picked up his car radio and advised everyone at the scene that he was going in alone. Neil would act as another customer, go inside, and look around. He opened the car door, stepped out and walked toward the glass front entrance.

There was no movement inside; Neil walked slowly, his eyes searching. He took out his handgun and inserted round into the chamber. Suddenly a man and a blonde woman appeared; they stood looking at a new vehicle in the showroom. Neil looked closer at the man it was Andy Bierkow. Tension, his only companion, dug its claws deeper into his shoulders, stiffening, burning. Neil opened the heavy, glass doors and stepped into the showroom. The woman looked away from the vehicle and looked at Neil, their eyes locking. Andy Bierkow totally attracted by the new car, was unaware of anything around him. The blonde woman, apparently a salesperson felt something strange, she kept looking at Neil, her eyes searching for an answer. Neil reached into his jacket and took out his identification.

"Andy Bierkow, I am with the FBI, we would like to ask you a few questions."

Without warning, a total fluid movement, Andy reached behind his back with his right arm and grabbed the blonde woman around the waist with his left, his right arm swung up holding a gun; he placed it under the woman's chin. In silence, he held the woman hostage, turning his head; he riveted his eyes on Neil. Three people stood waiting to see how fate would change their lives, the silence heavy, only muted traffic sounds filtered in from the street. It was a scene frozen in time.

A tiny sound started, high pitched, it resembled the distant keening of an animal in pain. Neil tried to identify the sound, he glanced at Andy and the blonde woman, they stood as if they were posing for a picture, his arm around her waist, a couple seemingly in love. The picture of the attractive couple an ugly illusion, Andy Bierkow held a handgun pressed under the blonde woman's chin, its muzzle buried in her skin, both of their eyes were wide, looking at Neil, waiting for his answer.

Motion started, the blonde woman's chest started to rise and fall, it seemed coordinated with the rise and fall of the keening sound. Neil saw the movement and instantly understood the increasing wail was the blonde woman's fear increasing. As the fear increased, the volume of the sound increased, now overwhelming the traffic sounds, filling the automobile dealership showroom.

Abruptly the wail stopped, the blonde-haired woman fainted from the traumatic stress. Neil could see the almost imperceptible sag to her body; her legs were not straight anymore. Andy Bierkow was holding the woman's unconscious body from falling to the floor. His posture was changing to compensate for the weight, Neil could see him leaning back slightly, Andy's arm had tightened its grip around the woman's waist, distorting and pulling her dress out of shape. Neither man spoke, silence solid between them, their eyes riveted together. Each man waited for the scales of fortune to tip in his favor.

The woman's weight took over the frozen scene, it overcame the hold Andy Bierkow had on her body, and she slowly started to slide to the floor. Andy totally focused on Neil was very unaware of the sensation she was leaving him exposed. It all happened so slowly.

The woman's head had reached the level of Andy's belt, her weight had dragged his gun down, no longer buried in her neck, and instead it angled down, the muzzle pointing at the floor. Andy Bierkow stood looking at Neil, his eyes wide and unmoving, unaware his upper torso was completely exposed, the woman no longer a hostage. The scales of fortune had tipped but not in his favor.

Neil's chest solid with tension, seemed to leave him no room to breathe. Training took over, curling his index finger around the trigger of his gun. It seemed he needed to fire the gun now in order to release his lungs and draw a breath of life. Andy Bierkow continued to stare at Neil; his eyes seemed to pierce into the depths of his soul, searching for something, an answer about the rest of his life.

An impasse reached; it seemed Neil had to fire his weapon in order to breathe again.

Two explosions from Neil's gun shattered the solid silence; the shots were so close together, they almost seemed like one. The left side of Andy Bierkow's chest blossomed into a red stain; he stood looking at Neil, waiting for an answer that would never come.

Fate is impatient and selfish it requires constant progress. It took away the breath of life holding Andy's body upright, slowly he and the woman started to sag toward the floor, his eyes never left Neil's eyes until he lay face down across the unconscious woman.

The sequence released Neil's lungs, life-giving air rushed into his mouth; it seemed to have a delicious flavor. Becoming aware of the surroundings, an ache in his hand radiated to his arm from the frozen grip on his gun. Training again took over; he relaxed his grip on the handgun, sliding it back into the holster. He was breathing heavily, his chest almost painful with the volumes of air expanding it. The feeling of Andy Bierkow's questioning eyes would stay with him forever. Neil's stress began to evaporate, and he felt extremely tired. His shots had triggered action from the SWAT team; he could hear them coming, their footsteps, and their voices.

It had been a long time since Neil had shot a suspect, it would take a long time to get over it, if ever. There were two traumatic memories to haunt him in the mornings, the loss of his wife's and this killing.

The ringing of his cell phone brought Neil back to total reality it was his office. He opened his cell phone and listened to a remote voice telling him good news. Apparently, there had been a call to the local police. A woman from a local bank had discovered a connection; there had been a money transfer to Hamid. She had a name of the client. Neil felt a needed rush of adrenaline.

Justification blossomed in his mind, he was right. His suspicions were right, there had been a central figure providing money and plans. The circle was slowly closing on the terror holding the city in its grasp.

As he snapped, the cell phone shut, the SWAT leader who had been standing beside him spoke, asking the routine questions following a shooting of a suspect. Neil responded with short, curt answers or just a shake of his head. He glanced at a member of the SWAT team crouched over Andy Bierkow's body, a finger on the suspect's neck, searching for a life-giving pulse. The member looked up at the Neil and his leader, he shook his head in a negative way, the suspect was dead. Another member moved over to help the kneeling man lift Andy's body off the unconscious woman. They picked Andy up by the armpits, leaving the woman's body exposed, covered in blood. Another member knelt down beside the woman, feeling her pulse, he too looked at Neil and his leader, he nodded, she was alive.

When SWAT starts, part of the group arriving on the scene is an ambulance, in case of shootings. The medics who had been waiting moved forward following a command by kneeling member. They knelt down on either side of the woman and began working their particular routine to bring her back.

Finally, the woman moved and with the assistance of the medics, she sat up, her chest starting to rise and fall rapidly with the intake of life-giving air. She looked around the showroom, her eyes wide, questioning, then she looked down the front of her dress and saw the blood, and she started screaming.

One of the medics reached into the bag on the floor beside him, he took out a syringe, took off the protective shield from the needle, he held the syringe upright, squirting some clear liquid into the air. The woman's screams rose in volume and she struggled with the other medic trying to restrain her. Finally, with extreme difficulty, the two men managed to extend her arm, pinning it. Her screams rose in volume, she struggled frantically. The medic with the syringe found the vein in her arm with little difficulty, he inserted the needle, and the sedative found its way into the woman. Response to the sedative was the abrupt cessation of her screams, then her struggles slowly subsided, the medics slowly helped her to stand upright. Her chest covered in blood, she stood and looked around the now crowded showroom, and there was total confusion in her eyes. Gently the medics took her by the arms and very slowly led her out of the showroom to the waiting ambulance.

SWAT members were everywhere, the situation under control. Neil's FBI colleagues were also present, standing beside him, their eyes wide, full of questions. Silent, his eyes averted, he slowly walked toward the door and his waiting car.

Neil had another circle to close; a master terrorist was still loose.

CHAPTER – 24

Carla sat stiff and tense in the interrogation room at the FBI headquarters. The pressure inside of her from anxiety and fear made her feel as if her whole body was ready to explode. She felt very conspicuous; the walls of room separating it from the hallway were glass. People were constantly glancing at her when they walked past the room. Their glances made her feel as if they knew everything, somehow they had found out about her and Saleem. Carla felt guilty, alone, ashamed and separated from the world, never so terrified in her whole life. She wondered why they were taking so long and what they would do to her. Anxiety was like a tortured beast inside of her, twisting and turning in agony.

Neil Chambers stood watching the lone woman; he was behind a one-way glass panel and not visible to her.

She was very nervous, glancing furtively at passing employees, constantly glancing repeatedly at the door to the room where she was contained. Her body karma seemed to radiate fear and anxiety. This woman had called the police regarding Hamid and a money transfer from another party, possibly a master terrorist. Neil stood for a long time watching, this was training procedure, it made suspects more vulnerable prior to interrogation. He wondered what the woman's story would be. Finally, glancing at his watch, Neil decided she was ready.

Carla had been sitting alone in the room so long, the tension inside of her was crackling, and she was so tense that she felt the door to the room opening. She looked up, fear rising like nausea into her throat. Would they want to know everything? If that was the case, it would expose her, she would lose her job, her dignity, and there would be no place to hide. The whole world would know she had been intimate with a terrorist. She had only microseconds to wonder why her life kept falling apart.

Neil entered the room and introduced himself; he could see the fear in the woman's widened eyes. She was certainly pretty, dressed low key, business like. A sudden thought flashed, resembling guilt, he wondered why he was noticing attractive women more. Taking a deep breath to drive away the needles of guilt, Neil walked around the table and sat across from Carla.

"I understand you have some information for us?" Emotional barriers' Carla built while she waited started to crumble. The man was attractive, soft spoken and he had a disarming air about him. Somehow, she felt vulnerable, attractive men constantly broke through her shields. She did not know how to start, the question was simple yet at this moment very complex, and Carla glanced down at her hands, the silence felt like a cage.

Neil looked at the woman, he had to tread carefully, she was acting like a frightened homemaker, yet her appearance radiated a businessperson, she should be confident.

What was wrong here?

Again, he tried very carefully, "you called the local police about some information about a suspect whose picture appeared on television. Can you give me some details?" Neil sat and waited for her silence to dissipate. Finally, Carla had extricated a path from all her confusion. It was a careful path; she would be comfortable to follow it. "I am employed by a downtown bank involved in international money transfers. A new client recently opened an account with us and deposited a considerable sum of money into the account. This is quite normal, we deal with clients all over the world, and a payment to a local individual combined with the picture on television prompted me to call the police." Carla waited, stress spreading like hot fire through her body.

Neil looked at the woman; she was looking down at her hands again. Something was wrong with the picture.

"Could this payment have been just a normal exchange for goods or services?" Neil was fishing for more information or a negative reaction from the woman.

"I have no way of knowing what transpired between these two men." Carla looked up at Neil, her eyes glancing off his, and then she looked back down at her hands again.

Neil could sense something was wrong, the body language of the woman was telling him she was very uncomfortable. It was time to ask the most important question. Fastening his gaze on Carla's head, Neil waited for her reaction. "Were you involved in anyway with this client?"

The question hit Carla hard she reacted instantly. In all her training and interaction with clients, eye contact was the key to all things; it was final test for truth. She had played the game with clients many times, her reaction lightening fast. Her job, her life, and her dignity were in the balance, this microsecond would be the rest of her life. When she looked up at the FBI agent, her insides were shaking; sudden claws of extreme stress dug into her shoulders, Carla Black performed the greatest feat of courage of her life. She looked up at Neil, her eyes locked with his and held. "I had no other dealings with the man other than routine bank business." She held his gaze, her very soul quivering. Seconds of fortune ticked away, then Neil looked away, he was satisfied, besides he could not exert such pressure on a woman.

"Can you provide us any more information on this man?" Neil sat waiting, she passed the true test, and she had looked at him with a constant gaze. Now it was just a basic information extraction process.

Carla knew the hotel where Saleem stayed, she knew his name of course, and it was just a matter of divulging the information to the FBI. She felt sudden guilt it resembled betraying a friend.

Saleem had been the first man in her life with gentleness and innocence, their lovemaking had been a journey into place very few people seldom reach. She could never forget his gentleness as long as she lived. Innocence also a flavor in man very few women ever experience. The FBI agent clearing his throat, when she looked up interrupted the rush of memories; he was looking at her intently.

"All the complete information is at my office, I call it into you?" Carla made her remark sound like a question; she needed emotional space to betray Saleem.

Neil and Carla locked eyes, hers did not waver, and he felt a closure from the questioning. There seemed to be something radiating from her, but she was willing to divulge the necessary information, the interview was over. He stood up and thanked Carla for her time and coming forward with possible information that could keep the people in the city safe from harm. He moved the short distance to glass door of the interview room, opened it and stood waiting for her to exit. "I will wait for your call," he said as he watched her walk gracefully down the hallway. Carla Black was an attractive woman; it reminded him how much he missed Ellen.

Dinner was just a token for Carla, leftovers from the fridge, she could feel the restlessness, and it followed her everywhere in the apartment. Walking back and forth, she would stray to the window and look at the day ending. Cloud formations had always been mystical to her, now she looked at them changing as evening progressed. She found only melancholy in their colors, sadness everywhere she looked. The day was ending, her life was in chaos, it seemed happiness had totally gone from her life. Carla Black sat in her favorite chair until darkness covered the landscape. She traveled emotionally to memories of her husband; there she found sharp edges and pain. Back to Saleem and the short-lived path that could have led to a fulfilling relationship, maybe even love.

Finally, she went back to bed, unable to sleep, Carla looked at the shadows in her bedroom, there had been no answer in her traditional cloud formations, and no answer existed in the shadows of the night. Sleep touched her softly but she drifted through tangled dreams, waking often, looking at the empty pillow and space on the other side of the bed. Depression began tugging at her, wanting her follow, it kept reminding her she was all alone in the city, and there was no one to hold her or comfort her. Morning came hard, it brought brutal reality, and her task lay hard and defined. Saleem had been part of something that harmed or killed innocent people. Her memories of him were soft and beautiful, but very short; Carla could not overcome her feelings of revulsion, only justice would drive it away. She stood for a long time watching the sunrise, the coffee her only friend, then abruptly she turned to make the fatal telephone call to the FBI.

CHAPTER - 25

Saleem woke early, a need kept nudging at him, making him restless. To do more acts of terrorism would be wrong at this time. The city was in chaos, police and FBI were in a frenzy to find the people responsible. The timing would be very bad at this time. In addition, he did not have any contacts to commit war against the Americans. Something was in his mind, so distant he could not distinguish it, it kept tugging at him. Saleem turned on his other side. He missed Carla, especially their intimacy. He had never experienced a physical connection with a woman; it left him very unsettled, hungry for more. Closing his eyes allowing the memories of her to play like a movie, Saleem remembered the first meeting in her office, she was a beautiful woman, and they had connected almost immediately. The memory movie played on, soft and warm, he remembered sitting across from Carla in her office, glancing at her hungrily.

Memories of their physical act suddenly came back around. Saleem lay in bed arousal flooding through his body, the need for Carla almost painful. He lay still and the many flavors of the intimate act came back, his need began creating plans. To stay in America would be good. Saleem knew his father carried a heavy burden of guilt for the years of hurt, he would provide a flow of money for as long as Saleem kept asking for more. He could start the business they planned; run the company and keep punishing America behind the scenes.

America was good; there were many luxuries, many beautiful women. It would be a good new life in an exciting new world.

His plans joined hands with all the memories in America, they danced for him, Carla came back, and his arousal came back. Saleem lay in bed drifting, enjoying, and thinking. He would see Carla again, his business would take him there, and his money account was set up with her. He did not understand why she had rejected him when he needed her very badly.

An exiting future lay ahead of him; the path was straight and full of promise. America had been good to him, full of promise. He would stay and do business and harm.

Saleem sat up in bed a thought came like lightning, bursting the bubble of all his good thoughts. The money transactions, payment to Hamid and Andy Bierkow, Carla would have a record of his name; she had seen Hamid on television. It hit him hard, he had not been careful, now he was vulnerable, the authorities could capture him, and it would be all over. Saleem's mind raced, and he understood why Carla had been cold and distant, she knew all about him. If she informed the police or the FBI, they would capture him.

His mind racing, stress heavy on his body, Saleem dal Figar lay in bed trying to find the opening to escape. All his dreams burst and scattered like startled birds into the sky, disappearing forever.

Plans of escape began to dance in his head, taking a flight out would be wrong, his passport was needed, his picture and name were on it. To drive south to Mexico would be fatal as it had been for Hamid. How could he leave without having to use his passport or pass through customs and immigration, was he trapped? The sadness of defeat began to trickle into his mind, weighing him down, and depression drifting in like grey clouds to destroy a sunny day.

The life saving thought came from the recesses of his memories; he suddenly remembered using a private jet in the family business in his homeland. If he chartered one, he would not have to pass through immigration, use his passport that had his betraying picture and name. He could fly to Mexico where immigration would not be looking for him. Energy flowed through him; he felt hope and life returning.

Saleem leaped out of bed, reached for the telephone, and called the front desk, advising them to close his accounts; he would be leaving this morning. Looking through the telephone book, he found a listing for charters; they asked for his credit card number, it would assure him they would hold a Lear for his arrival. The shower was just a token; Saleem rushed to dress, filling his suitcase with only the necessities for survival. The elevator ride to the front lobby seemed exceptionally slow this morning, anxiety rode his shoulders like a heavy beast.

The lobby was a beehive of activity, people arriving from the airport, people like Saleem impatiently waiting to check out and leave on the airport limousine. When he arrived, they were ready for him, all the necessary paper a simple formality, a signature, a call to the valet and his BMW was waiting at the front entrance.

He turned from the front desk; his checkout completed and heard a man standing further down. "Do you have someone registered here by the name of Saleem dal Figar?" A clerk looked on the computer and did not find Saleem's name, he had registered under a company credit card. He looked up at Neil Chambers and shook his head in a negative way, I'm sorry sir, there is no one staying here by that name."

Saleem knew Carla had betrayed him, an emotional door closed on a beautiful woman in his life, he would never see her again, a transient sadness passed through him, dissipating when he opened the trunk of his BMW. Placing his suitcase in the trunk, Saleem opened the front driver's door, sat in the driver's seat, and without looking, turned the car away from the hotel.

The Lear Jet rose into the morning sky, its wings riding the pacific air currents. Saleem sat back, his problems now on the ground far below, he felt like the plane, free of the ground, heading toward a new future, his experiences to guide him.

Neil Chambers stood in the hotel lobby, many unanswered questions buzzing through his head. They had no picture of the master terrorist, nothing to go on, just a name that could be false.

His immediate future promised no rest, he was committed to capturing the person responsible for the horrendous loss of human life, destruction, and chaos in the city.

Somehow, he would find that individual.